REMEMBERING

Books in the Valley of Artisans Series
by AmyLu Riley

Remembering

Open for Miracles

A Winter Wedding in the Valley of Artisans

Ordinary Miracles

Join the email list
https://amylu-riley.com/subscribe

REMEMBERING

AmyLu Riley

Published by
AmyLu Riley
Evansville, Indiana
United States of America
https://amylu-riley.com

Remembering: Valley of Artisans – Book 1

Published by AmyLu Riley
Evansville, Indiana, United States of America
books@amylu-riley.com

ISBN: 9781956738001 (paperback)
ISBN: 9781956738018 (ebook)
Library of Congress Control Number: 2021919460

First Edition, 2021

Cover design: Richard Riley
Cover photos: AmyLu Riley, Richard Riley, Mikaela Wiedenhoff, Anthony Ievlev, Geronimo Giqueaux, Liv Cashman, Khurt Williams, Joanna Kosinska, Luann Hunt, Olivia Spink, Griffin Wooldridge
Author photo: Richard Riley

Typefaces: Sorts Mill Goudy, Libre Franklin SemiBold, Josefin Sans, Lovers Quarrel, Old Standard TT

Printed in the United States of America.

Acknowledgements

I would like to thank my husband, Richard Riley, and my family and friends for your love, encouragement, and support of my writing. I thank God for you.

Chapter One

RIVER CARTER HAD never liked goat cheese, until she finally tried it. And now she could not eat a fresh peach or a spinach salad without thinking about how well goat cheese went with either one, and how all goat cheese really *lacked* was a more appetizing name.

However, as she rolled her bike down the driveway toward the mailbox, she realized with some disappointment that *she* lacked the cheese itself, because she had forgotten to buy any yesterday during her grocery run. Her spinach salad would just have to carry on for dinner tonight without her favorite topping.

River briefly wondered if there might be space here in the yard at Grandma's house—well, *her* house, now—to keep an actual goat. Not that she would have time for a pet with all she was about to embark on. Maybe there'd be time for a pet of some kind later, she told herself, but definitely not now.

Holding her bike's handlebars with one hand, River flipped open the door of the mailbox. *E. Carter* it read in black script on the side of the large metal box, amidst a swirl of painted green and white moonflower vines and flowers.

She would have to find out if the artist who had painted the mailbox mural was still here in the Valley. She would like to have her own first initial put on the mailbox, and maybe have some vines of blue morning glory added to the design while she was at it.

Empty. Maybe she had already gotten the mail today, she thought, as a hummingbird zinged toward her on its way to the front flowerbed for its evening meal, then stopped in midair, hung there, and peered at her face.

Here's something new, its gaze seemed to say.

The bird was stunning, and River stared back. Its jeweled green feathers shimmered even more brilliantly than the metallic glaze she loved to use on her pottery.

"Hello, sweetie," she said in a gentle, friendly tone to the thumb-sized creature. "I'm River. I live here now. May I call you Emerald?"

The little bird seemed to consider her for another split second before zipping off into the shelter of a nearby tree.

Well, River thought, getting onto her bike and pedaling into the road, *that's the kind of pet I'll have time for.*

❧

When she reached the top of the low rise where Great-Aunt Della's house and café had stood River's entire life, River stopped her bike in the road and just drank in the picture.

The structure looked a little bit like something transported from a European village, but she knew that her great-uncle, Della's brother Jim, had built it—and the guest house behind it—himself, right here on this spot in what he called *God's Country*, in southern Indiana.

In River's family, everything south of Indianapolis seemed to be considered *southern*

Indiana. And River remembered wondering as a young child why Uncle Jim felt that the top half of the state should be excluded from God's special favor. It was one of those mysteries that River had pondered as a girl but neither solved nor inquired about, so it had just been filed away in some drawer in the back of her mind, along with a million other things.

As she stood there astride the bicycle on Lantern Ridge Road, drinking in the perfect weather and the profuse flowerbeds that spilled color over half of Aunt Della's front yard, she thought how funny it was that that particular obscure childhood memory about her great-uncle should present itself to her now.

Even though River was mostly recovered from a toxic mold exposure that had caused neurological symptoms, her memory could still be like a hummingbird at times, arriving—or flitting away—entirely on its own terms. One could no more direct it than one could summon a hummingbird. If she *could*, she would request that it save and produce useful pieces of information—like remembering to buy goat cheese and recalling that she'd already gotten the mail today—instead of offering her spontaneously retrieved, decades-old facts she had no need of, such as the name of the old man from her childhood church who had always worn suspenders.

"You might as well laugh as cry," Grandma had been known for saying. And laugh is exactly what River had decided to do.

And now that she was doing much better, River's family had encouraged her to make the move here and take over the potter's wheel that her grandmother had always promised would one day be hers.

Of course, it was more than just the wheel. Being here also meant running the shop and participating as an active member of the artisan community—helping to organize festivals and events for visitors, and generally doing her part to help make the Valley of Artisans a thriving tourist destination.

For all of the shop owners here, their craft was their number-one love. But, as her great-uncle had once remarked, "As long as you have the habit of eating, you're going to need to make money."

Tourists had once flocked in large numbers to the many shops here, and the artisans who remained in the Valley hoped those numbers would surge again. Many of the original craftspeople had retired and closed their shops, while others carried on just as they always had. Some, like River, represented a younger generation who were now stepping into the shoes—and shops—of their elders. They all had a lot of work ahead of them to once again make the Valley of Artisans a thriving tourist destination, delighting visitors and thereby feeding the makers' habits of both creating art and taking meals at regular intervals.

River waved and smiled genially as a departing café customer got into a small car parked on the street and pulled away. She didn't recognize the driver. River pedaled up to the café's ground floor porch and public entrance, and stowed her bike, leaning it against the painted bench. As she stepped inside and pushed the wood door shut, the delicious scents of her great-aunt's cooking greeted her.

"River, honey! I thought it was about time we'd be seeing you." Aunt Della came around the counter and enfolded River in a big hug.

A few feet away, at a sturdy, dark wooden table, Uncle Jim was finishing a plate of fish. He smiled at River and swallowed an entire mouthful of food in one gulp. "Hello there, stranger," he said, getting up to give her a hug.

"Would you like a plate of the special?" Aunt Della asked. "I ate earlier between customers and Jim's just finishing up, but there's plenty for you in the warmer."

Della's cooking was legendary in the Valley, but twilight was already falling and River didn't like to bicycle in the dark, so she declined, with a promise to come back to the café soon and join them for a meal.

Aunt Della reached into her pocket and pulled out a key on a painted leather keychain that was made to look like a sandal. River had seen her grandmother use that same key many times to unlock the pottery shop. Della handed it over to River now, without any fanfare, as if it were the most natural thing in the world that River should now be the owner of both the shop and its former proprietor's key.

"How is the unpacking going at the house? Do you need anything?" Aunt Della asked. "Did you forget anything important?"

"It actually went pretty quickly," River said, zipping the shop key securely inside her bag. "In fact, I'm pretty much finished at the house for now. And I stopped for groceries on my way into town this morning, so I think I have everything I need at the moment, but thanks. Well, everything except the goat cheese I forgot to put on the list, but I can live without that." River laughed. "If it's not on the list, it doesn't have a chance."

Aunt Della laughed her rich, broad laugh. "Well, my sister always said, '*Forgetting* may be out of your hands, but *forgiving* is always in reach.'"

River laughed. "That sounds like something Grandma would have put on one of her signs."

Jim snorted appreciatively at this apt characterization of his and Della's beloved sister's penchant for sayings, and a mouthful of coffee tried to escape through his nose.

"Well, I can't think of anyone I need to forgive," said River. "But then," she added with a playful smile, "I *usually* can't think of anything I've forgotten."

Chapter Two

AS THE MORNING sun did its best to burn through the bedroom curtains, River stood on the opposite side of the room and ran her hand across the clothes she had hung the day before in the small closet of her new, but very old, home. What, she wondered, was the right sort of thing to wear for the first day of the rest of one's life?

She would be attending a meeting of the Artisans' Guild this morning, and she wanted to look presentable for that, but she would also be cleaning at the pottery shop that had been closed for too long. She decided that the day's agenda was too much to ask of any one outfit. She would dress for the meeting, and take along a change of clothes.

She pulled out a pair of blue linen pants and a matching top. The outfit required ironing every time it was washed, so she never selected it lightly. Ironing meant just that many minutes of one's life that one would never get back. But this occasion seemed like a worthy one.

Once that task was done, and the outfit had already been wrinkled by the mere act of putting it onto a body with bendable arms and legs, River tucked her work clothes into her well-worn leather bag, along with a notebook and some pens. She planned to take meticulous notes during the meeting, not the least of which would be writing down everyone's names.

To help rebuild the tourism that had once been the lifeblood of the Valley, the Artisans' Guild wanted to bring the seasonal festivals back to the level of their former glory. Today's session was the first meeting to make a collective plan for doing just that.

River was excited about the idea. She remembered those festivals from her childhood. She knew how much everyone—residents and visitors alike—had enjoyed those occasions. And now, as the owner of a pottery shop, she also realized how important they would be for the profitability of her business and that of the other artisans' shops, as well.

She pulled the backpack-style straps of her bag up onto her shoulders, snapped on her bike helmet, and walked out to the garage. A first-day-of-school kind of feeling washed over River—a feeling of anticipation, combined with that empty space one's stomach makes for the unknown when one is irrevocably headed into it.

Chapter Three

A WOMAN CALLED Natalie with a perpetual smile and long, dark hair in a messy bun called the Artisans' Guild meeting to order with a casual, "Hey, everybody, grab a chair, we'd better get started."

Natalie was a jewelry maker who ran two shops in town. In one, she made jewelry. In another, she had crafting stations where customers could design and assemble their own jewelry using beads, baubles, and doodads they selected from the rows of bins provided.

There was a loud sound of metal folding chairs dragging across the concrete basement floor of the Valley of Artisans Community Center, as the makers assembled themselves in a circle.

River immediately spotted an older woman whom she thought she remembered being the mural painter she was looking for. She jotted a note on page 2 of her notebook, *Talk to mural painter about mailbox,* and then flipped back to page 1, where she planned to write down names as people were introduced. She would draw a circle on the paper and write each person's name in a spot corresponding with where they sat at this meeting. Faces she could remember, but her notes would have to do the rest.

Thankfully, Natalie began the meeting by asking everyone to introduce themselves since there were several new people in the group.

A man next to River about her age with a gentle voice introduced himself as Danny. He said he was the grandson of the original owner of his family's woodworking shop in the Valley. River remembered seeing Danny's grandfather outside the woodworking shop during festivals of her childhood, carving a bear out of a log with a chainsaw, while tourists stood and gaped and drank in the smell of wood. Danny said he and his wife Kate had recently moved here to take over the shop. So, Danny and Kate were third-generation shop owners now, just as she was.

River introduced herself as Ella Carter's granddaughter, the new owner of the pottery shop.

"I think I remember your brother," said Danny. "Don't you have a brother named Nick?"

"That's right," said River, nodding.

"Okay," said Danny thoughtfully, recognition dawning. "I think I remember you, now, too."

The group didn't seem to mind this little foray into neighborliness. River knew from hearing her family's stories over the years that the arts community here was generally made up of some quite friendly people—and a few curmudgeons.

Like Mr. Lyle, the broom-squire. He and River's Grandma Ella had gone to school together. Grandma used to say that he drank from the pickle juice. That had been Ella Carter's catchall rationale for any occurrence of sour demeanor.

And then there was Mrs. Hayes. She had run the antique mall at the edge of town for decades, because every tourist destination seemed to need one of those. But she had never liked antiques—or tourists. She referred to her expansive inventory dismissively as *that old junk*, and her favorite time of the day seemed to be closing time, when she could escape the sprawling building crammed with other people's nostalgia.

There were others, too, River knew. No village was quite as idyllic as the Artisans' Guild hoped to make this one feel to tourists. But they were sure going to try.

When it came time for the woman River recognized as the mural painter to introduce herself, River quickly noted her name, *Sara*, on the notepad in her lap, before allowing herself to take a longer look. Sara's artsy outfit made River think of a character from one of her favorite children's books—a woman who wore garments one really couldn't figure out well enough to describe them. That was just the sort of attire that one could expect in a group of creatives like this, and it didn't seem pretentious or out of place here. These people were working artists. Their clothes were sometimes an expression of their art, and, sometimes, just something they covered themselves with so they could get on with making their art.

As the introductions continued around the circle, River continued to note names and businesses. Anna was an herbalist who kept the herb shop, and River recognized the woman as being her next-door neighbor.

The variety of businesses represented should be enticing to tourists, River thought. A long time ago, the Valley had given up trying to have a separate commerce organization for the businesses that weren't strictly artisan businesses. Now, most of the business owners in the Valley were members of the Artisans' Guild, and it seemed to work fine. They all wanted the same thing: tourists and customers.

Some of the owners, like her great-aunt and great-uncle, were stretched too thin to attend meetings, but were happy to go along with what the other members decided. "No, honey, the food here won't cook or serve itself," Aunt Della had laughed, when River had asked if she or Uncle Jim would be at the meeting.

As Natalie guided the meeting through the various points of discussion on the agenda, other shopkeepers gave a rundown of the challenges the

Guild members faced. So many problems. More than River had realized.

Such a large number of shops had closed that the remaining Guild members had stopped holding the seasonal festivals. But that, it turned out, had hurt business even more. The Guild members now agreed that they needed to revive the seasonal festivals in order to once again make the Valley of Artisans an appealing tourist destination—and make a living for themselves. The first order of business: to revive AutumnFest this coming fall, in order to attract visitors during that important tourism season.

Not only would the seasonal festivals need to make a comeback, however. The Guild members also wanted create a collective online presence. This would go beyond the individual online businesses of their respective stores. It would be a way to build online the same kind of excitement that the physical festivals did. After all, many people who appreciated handcrafted items and wanted to buy them might never actually *come* to Valley of the Artisans. It was time to take the shops to them.

As River slowly pedaled away from the meeting toward the pottery shop, her mind was so full that she didn't even notice the scenery around her. Until the meeting this morning, River hadn't realized the state of the tourism business in the Valley, and how much work was going to be needed to revitalize business. She saw clearly now how much she would need the Guild's plans to work. Not only would the pottery shop be her own source of income, but it was also her *dream* to make and sell pottery the way her grandma had taught her.

Without a vision, the people perish. Well, this was her vision, and she intended to flourish as a person. The shop *had* to succeed, not just because it had been Grandma's legacy to her, but because this was her dream. She might have to use lists and notes as memory aids to make the business succeed, but she *would* do it.

The Valley's business problems would be addressed one layer at a time, she told herself, just like her own healing had been—like peeling the layers of an onion. The news at the meeting admittedly hadn't been rosy, but River was committed to doing everything she could to help the Artisans' Guild's plans succeed, starting with setting up an online store for her pottery shop and stocking it and her physical shop with the kind of pieces that turned browsing into buying—and Valley of Artisans tourists into repeat customers. She would do her part to make the festival and the Guild's website a success, too.

All of this would take a lot of her time, but that was okay. River really didn't have anything to distract her. No other ties or commitments vied for her time and attention.

This was her life now. And she was ready to throw herself in with both feet, or jump in over her head, or whatever the saying was.

❧

After spending the rest of the day cleaning at the shop, River was more than ready to fall into her bed. She had been glad for a shower and a simple dinner, and could almost hear her pillow calling. She answered its summons as soon as she had cleaned up the kitchen and sent her family some texts.

River: Hey, bro. Shop looks just like always. Spent the day cleaning. Tired puppy. How are you?
Nick: Hey, Riv. Be weird if it didn't, I guess. I'm good. School's good. Never chopped so many onions in my life.
River: Still have all 10 fingers?
Nick: Lol. Yes, at last count.
River: Excellent. A+, you. Love ya. Nite.
Nick: Thanks. Love ya. Nite.

River: Hey, Mom. How are you guys?
Mom: Hi! Good here. How did it go today?
River: Alright. Guild meeting was an eye-opener. Lotta work ahead.
Mom: One day at a time. Don't forget to sleep.
River: Yep. Love you. Good night.
Mom: Love you, too. Good night.

A few minutes later, River gratefully rested her head on the cotton pillow. But as the welcome twilight sleep began to wash over her, something else most unexpectedly came in with that tide.

Chapter Four

HANNAH HAD BEEN one of River's first college roommates and the two had quickly become best friends. Over the four years that River and Hannah had roomed together in college, they had regularly visited each other's families during holidays and school breaks, and always thoroughly enjoyed their time together.

From the time Hannah and River had first met, Hannah's father had been seriously ill, and over the years, his health had had its ups and downs. But then, during fall midterms week of their senior year, his health had suddenly turned sharply south and he had died.

Hannah had made it home in time to say goodbye to her dad, but River, of course, had to stay at school to take her midterm exams. There was no excused absence from college midterm exams for a friend of the family, the way there was for a daughter.

But when Hannah had come back to their shared room at school, it had been for just long enough to pack up her things. Hannah said that she had requested a housing reassignment.

River had been so surprised that she had just stood dumbly and looked into her friend's face while Hannah talked. Hannah had said that River hadn't been there for her during her dad's illness, and that she didn't want the kind of friend who wasn't going to be there for her when she really needed her.

River had been stunned. Where else had she *been* during his illness besides with Hannah? The two had been together most of the time for the entire four years they had known each other. River wondered what more she could possibly have done.

But the answer, as River lay on her bed in the dark in her house in the Valley, was still the same tonight as it had been years ago when she had first considered the question: *It didn't matter.* Hannah had been hurt, and whether or not it made sense to River *how* she had failed, she had somehow let her friend down when it had mattered most.

The return of this latent memory had brought to River more than just an objective replay of events.

As she turned her head on her pillow, she realized that the fabric was wet, and that her cheeks were wet. And her heart and her head hurt in an old way that, although it had been forgotten for a long time, now felt quite familiar.

Chapter Five

AN UNTRAINED PUPPY, thought River, would have been less disruptive than the tidal wave of memory that had crashed into her last night. And much more fun.

She hadn't slept much, and what sleep she had managed to get had seemed more like work than rest. And then it had been time to get up.

With some effort, River tried to focus her bleary eyes on the names of the various herbal teas in the assortment box. *Just pick the pink one*, she told herself. *The pink one is rose, and the smell of roses always makes you feel better.*

But as good as the tea, and her entire morning routine of exercise, prayer, Bible reading, journaling, and breakfast, were, River did not feel better.

The old memory of the scene with Hannah continued to bob persistently at the surface of her mind, like a buoy on the water, and River found herself unable to dismiss it.

It broke through her thoughts as she went about every part of her day. Even as she leaned over her laptop at a small table at the pottery shop, trying to focus on an action plan for starting a business website, there was the old memory, insistently demanding her attention.

River finally gave up trying to do anything that required her focus, and returned to cleaning the shop.

Something felt urgent about this memory—like she needed to *do* something about it. But that seemed odd, for a years-old event to require an immediate response. River wondered why now, and what kind of response that would even be.

Those questions would go unanswered.

Chapter Six

THE MEMORY CONTINUED to permeate River's mind while she slept that night. She awoke again the following morning with the exhausted feeling of having been awake all night, even though she knew she had not been.

This wasn't going to work. Something would have to be done, but River did not know what.

I really have a lot on my plate right now, God. I need to be able to sleep, and to focus on my work.

You know I've tried to contact Hannah before, and she doesn't want to hear from me. I have made an attempt in good faith to apologize. What more can I do? Can't I be free from the nagging sense that I need to do more, when there's nothing more I can do?

River resolved she would not worry about it, but would tell God what she needed, like Philippians 4 said to do. Wasn't that the way to experience peace?

After all, it wasn't reasonable to go on a wild goose chase after every little thing from the past. Who knew what might come tumbling out of her recovered memories next; it was unpredictable. And she had things to do: urgent, important things that had to do with living her life right now—not old matters, forgotten by everyone in the world except, apparently, her.

This memory was nothing more than part of the past, and it could remain there. It just needed to settle back down into its place and go back to sleep, like an old dog on a comfortable rug in front of a fireplace. It didn't need to be taken on a hike up a mountain.

Chapter Seven

BY THE END of that week, the shop was as clean as it was ever going to be. River had used the old cobweb broom, no doubt made decades before by Mr. Lyle, to clear all of the high corners. She had washed down every surface and shelf, and wiped down every piece of pottery that remained on the shelves.

She had been pleasantly surprised to find that there were still several boxes of inventory in the back, as well as the many pieces already on display.

Grandma had made some stunning pottery, and it made River smile to handle these beautiful bowls, pitchers, mugs, plates, and the myriad other creative works that Ella Carter had gladly poured her life into.

River had always loved this shop, from the time she was a girl. River knew that what she felt wash over her whenever she stepped into this building was love. Ella might be gone, but the love she had shared with her family, and in her art, was not.

Sitting in the workroom at the shop, eating her tuna salad on a bed of baby spring greens, River wondered whether it would be better to get all of the new pieces made first that she'd need to fully stock the shop in time for AutumnFest, or whether she should focus on setting up the new website first in order to begin trying to get some online sales.

By the time she had finished her salad and unwrapped her peanut butter cookie from its waxed paper, River had made some decisions. She would focus solely on the website for now, and she would use Grandma's remaining inventory to stock the store for AutumnFest.

She flipped open the lid of her laptop computer, and plugged in the external mouse. It was time to get this website show on the road.

Now she just had to figure out exactly how to do that.

Chapter Eight

THE VALLEY OF ARTISANS Master Gardeners had erected a gazebo at the end of the street that was not only a stunning central focus for their display garden, but was also an ideal shaded location in which to eat lunch outdoors on summer days when the southern Indiana temperature didn't begin with a 9 or a 10. So, over the next two weeks, River did so regularly.

On the stretch of street between the pottery shop and the gazebo was a row of several of the Valley's original shops, including the woodworking shop. River developed the habit of stopping in at the woodworking shop on her way to lunch, just long enough to say hello to Danny and Kate. They were as busy as she was with trying to get a new website up, while Danny also worked to create the kinds of handmade wood pieces they thought would most appeal to tourists and online shoppers.

"Hey, there!" said Kate, looking up from her computer as River stuck her head in the door one day on her way to lunch.

"Hi, how's it going with the website?" River asked.

"I'm not even sure how to answer that," laughed Kate. "It seems like everything I go to do, requires something else that I haven't done yet, so I have to backtrack and do that thing, except that thing requires something else I haven't done yet, and so on. I have had one task on my to-do list now for three days, and I have spent all day every single day trying to complete all the various steps it's going to take just to get that one thing done, and I'm still not done with it."

River laughed.

"Okay, well at least I know I'm not alone. That's about how mine is going, too, so I feel your pain."

"Hey, I know we're all working overtime to get ready for AutumnFest," Kate said, "But why don't you come over some night this week for dinner at our house? Danny loves to fire up the grill, and we could have burgers or something."

It sounded nice. Fun even. And River really liked Kate and Danny. It would be good to have some friends here.

"Oh, I would love to," said River, pausing as she caught herself, "but I'm going to have to take a raincheck on that. Thank you, though. It sounds great. Maybe we can do it later sometime."

Kate responded cheerfully.

"Okay, definitely. Well, hang in there. We'll all get through this website stuff, and live to tell the stories." She smiled.

River returned Kate's friendly smile, wished them a good afternoon, and headed to the gazebo to eat her lunch. She expected that she would *live* to tell, but she was also pretty sure no one would ever want to *hear* the website stories she was living.

Website creation seemed tedious to her. It was nothing like clay, which one could transform from a wet lump to a form of beauty by the skilled performance of one's hands. Instead, it was typing and more typing. Tap, tap, tap. The only feeling under her hands as she worked on the site was that of the square plastic keys on the keyboard. If she wanted to make a shape, or words, or anything else appear on the website, those keys were the small doors her ideas had to crawl through on their bellies to get there.

And not only did she need to get her own website with its online store up and running, but she also had to do her part to help with the Guild's festival website.

This is how business was done, she knew. It was necessary. She would just be glad when the website projects were behind her.

She had to give the Guild credit—she thought the concept for the festival website was a good one. It would feature an artist's rendition of the Valley—complete with every actual shop that was participating. When a website visitor clicked on a shop—for example, the pottery shop—they would then see a virtual storefront window with a photo of a showcased item for sale, plus a 360-degree video tour of the inside of the shop, and a link to visit that shop's full website. The whole thing would be great for promoting all of the businesses in the Valley for all of the seasonal festivals, and year-round, as well.

River wondered how she should go about selecting which of her pieces of pottery to feature in the prime spots of her own website's home page and on the festival website.

Grandma Ella's best-sellers had always been mugs. Even tourists with a cabinet full of mugs at home wanted to buy more mugs as souvenirs, or as gifts. And Grandma's mugs had all the special touches that seemed to make them irresistible. There were the thumbprint mugs, with a rest at the top of the handle for a weary thumb. And the untippable glazed mugs with their bulging flares at the bottom, perfect for using near computers or children. And the heavy relief mugs, with sculpted designs on the sides, making them so irresistibly artsy looking that they had turned many a browser into a buyer.

But the mugs weren't the highest profit-margin item, River knew. The complete sets of dishes were. A set of eight dinner plates, salad plates, bowls, and matching mugs—those were the sales that really brought in the income.

But how many tourists could reasonably be expected to buy a complete set of dishes?

Wouldn't it be better to tout a lower priced item that more people might be more likely to buy? As she finished her tuna salad and headed back to her shop, River wondered which was better in the long run. Should she even be focused on short-term profit? Or was it better to promote pieces that would create repeat business and word-of-mouth promotion?

River was curious whether the owners of the businesses she passed on her way all knew what they were doing when it came to matters like these, or if everyone in the Guild asked themselves these same kinds of questions.

Chapter Nine

ON HER LUNCH break the next day, River ventured to the gallery.

The inside of Sara's place felt as peaceful as swimming underwater. Her many paintings—oils and watercolors—hung in rows on the high walls of the front room, and the peace of the place seemed to soak into River's skin as she stood and looked around her.

A large back room held artwork of a different kind, murals painted on sections of old barnwood and on lengths of old wooden fences. These had the expansive playfulness of fields of flowers, or of bright and cheery bird scenes, or an entire beach—the latter being something one would never see in real life in the Valley of Artisans, but Sara didn't let that stand in the way of her art.

As Sara came out of her workroom to greet her visitor, she recognized River and gave her a warm smile.

"How's the new potter doing?" Sara asked.

"I think I may completely forget how to throw pottery by the time I get these website projects done," River laughed.

"Oh, that won't do," Sara replied with a kind smile, shaking her head.

"I agree," said River. "Thankfully, I still have inventory from my Grandma Ella to stock the shop in the meantime."

"Oh, so it's not all 'out with the old, in with the new'?"

"No, no. Although, there is one update I'd like your help with making, if you still do mural painting on location."

River told Sara about her vision for the mailbox mural at the house, and asked if Sara would have time to even consider such a project.

Sara seemed glad for the invitation to freshen up the old mural that she confirmed she had originally painted years ago for Ella Carter. She said if River didn't mind her fitting it in between other things, and didn't have a hard deadline for its being finished, she'd take on the project. Ella had been a good woman, Sara said. River smiled appreciatively and gladly agreed to Sara's terms.

River realized that Sara must know nearly everyone in the Valley of Artisans, and an idea occurred to her.

"You wouldn't happen to know anyone who could help me with writing product descriptions for my pottery website, would you?"

Sara thought for a minute, pursing her lips and rolling her eyes up to that place where names are recovered from thin air.

"I'm not sure whether she'd want to do writing for a website, but you could ask Vera Stanford. She's been writing for a long time. Maybe she could help you."

After getting some contact information for Vera, River thanked Sara for her help, and crossed the expansive wooden floor of Sara's peaceful shop to the door, whose latch made a discreet metallic click behind her as the tiny bell above it politely announced her departure.

Sara had seemed so kind, so grounded, so real, that River had briefly thought of asking if she would like to get coffee sometime. It *would* be nice to make some friends here. But River had let the idea pass. She could visit Aunt Della and Uncle Jim when she had the time to socialize with anyone.

For now, she needed to stay focused on the task before her.

Maybe she would contact Vera to ask her about writing for the website. Some well-crafted, enticing descriptions of the pottery pieces should help sales. River could envision creative pottery pieces and make them come to life from clay and glaze, but she knew that describing them was another art form altogether—and not one she had mastered.

Chapter Ten

FOR THREE WEEKS, River had tried to ignore the elephant in the room of her heart and move on. She had gone about her business, eating and breathing and working. But she hadn't slept well.

Instead of her normal focus and peace and creativity and rest, she had felt scattered and fragmented, wrung-out, and restless. The persistent idea that she needed to *do* something about the long-ago situation with Hannah hadn't receded. But she really had no idea what that *something* might be. She hadn't been in touch with Hannah in years. And even if she had a way to contact her, what would the point be? River really didn't understand at all why she hadn't just been able to drop this.

And then, one evening, River realized that her inability to forget the matter wasn't coming from *her* at all—it was a prompting from the Holy Spirit.

She didn't want to quench the Spirit. She wanted to keep in step with the Spirit. But what did God want her to do?

God, I want peace. But I don't know what you want me to do. Please show me what to do.

And then, in response, River heard nothing. She got no impressions. She had no inspired ideas.

She brushed her teeth with her old electric toothbrush that really needed a new head on it, put on her pajamas, and got into bed. She hoped for a good night's sleep, but, at this point, expected it would probably just be another restless night.

❧

That night, River had two dreams.

In the first one, she saw fingers going through a filing cabinet. It seemed like the filing cabinet was hers, but the fingers were not.

Then the scene changed, and she saw two sets of footprints—one was inside the other—leading to a whiteboard. She wanted to see what was written on the whiteboard. But when she reached it, there was nothing on it.

❧

The next morning, as River made herself a coconut kefir smoothie, she checked her email on her phone—something she usually never did until the rest of her morning routine was complete. She saw that Vera Stanford had returned her email inquiry about writing for the website, and that she was available this afternoon, as well as some other times, to meet with River to discuss the idea.

River immediately replied to confirm the time Vera had suggested for that afternoon, and to ask for the address of Vera's home, where Vera had suggested they meet.

God seemed unusually quiet to River that morning. She prayed. She sketched out the Scripture she read. But she heard nothing, and neither did anything from the Scripture seem to rise up to meet her.

And then she finished getting ready and bicycled to her shop, where she continued at her website tasks, which felt to her like hacking a path through a massive jungle with a small machete.

❧

After lunch, eaten without a break from working, River put her laptop in her bag, and rode to the address Vera had given her. As soon as she saw the house, she realized that she had been here before. This was the home of her grandma's best friend. Her grandma had always called her friend Vivi, and so River had not made the connection, not recognizing the name Vera Stanford.

River parked her bike in the driveway and exhaled a long breath. She relaxed at the thought of being in the company of someone she knew she could trust—someone Grandma Ella had trusted so completely.

Vera held open the front door of the cottage-style home. The attractive wood front door with its rounded top reminded River vaguely of the houses in Hobbiton, but there the similarity ended, for Vera was tall and she wore shoes—on human-sized feet.

"I'm glad you're here," said Vera comfortably as she welcomed her guest.

"I just realized that you are Vivi," River laughed. "I put two-and-two together when I saw your house and remembered being here with Grandma."

Vera nodded and smiled. "Yes, and I don't even know how Ella came to give me that nickname, but she never called me anything else."

"Well, I'm glad to be here. Thank you for having me."

"Why don't we go into the kitchen and have a glass of lemonade? I've been working in my study all day and I'm ready for a change of scenery and a different chair."

"That sounds good," said River, as she followed behind Vera.

River sat down at the wooden table with its two drop leaves and noticed a sign over the door leading to the back porch that said *PRAY WITHOUT CEASING*. She wondered briefly if her grandma had made the sign for Vera. And then she wondered, as she always had about that particular Scripture, how it was even possible to do what the words said.

As Vera mixed water, lemon juice, and honey into a pitcher and poured it over ice in two glasses, she asked River about her new life in the Valley.

River found herself opening up to this woman in a way she normally would not. Instead of giving the *everything's-great* answer, she surprised herself by saying, "So far, it's not what I expected. I thought I would be making pottery and selling it to customers, but it seems like all I've been doing is working on marketing materials and not sleeping very well."

Vera nodded with understanding as she listened and watched River's eyes. Although the woman said nothing for a few moments, it didn't feel like a lull in the conversation. It felt as if something was happening in the silent space she was creating.

And maybe it was.

A younger River had soaked in enough kitchen-table conversations between her late grandmother and this woman to know that Vera wasn't like most other people.

River remembered that when Vera prayed—which she had done often and quite naturally as she talked with Grandma Ella—there was a calm authority in her words. She carried a power, mingled with humility, that River had never tried to describe, but that was still here—it was undeniable. She recalled how matter-of-factly Vera had spoken to her best friend Ella about visions and prophecies, as if those things happened every day.

In short, Vera expected the impossible to arise from childlike faith and obedience to God, and around her, it did. But she was never arrogant or strange about any of it. She was an earthy, real person who just seemed to be living a different kind of life than most. It intrigued River.

"And your email indicated that you're looking for some writing help for your marketing materials?"

Vera's gentle remark brought River back to the conversation.

"Yes," River said. "I'd like to have some descriptions for the various pottery pieces on my website. Artsy descriptions that will help sell them."

As their lemonade glasses grew emptier, River's hopes rose. Vera asked questions about how many and what kind of pieces would be featured and about her ideas for conveying the artistry and functionality of the various pottery on offer.

River opened her laptop to show Vera the unpublished website and explained that, initially, all of the pieces on offer would be those that Grandma Ella had made. "Of course, I'll be adding my own pottery as soon as I can spend some time at the wheel," River said.

River noticed that as she spoke, Vera seemed to grasp not only her words, but also much more than River was saying. But rather than this seeming like an intrusion, River felt seen and understood by the older woman.

"This isn't my typical line of work these days," said Vera with a smile, "but I'll be happy to help you."

Something loosened in River's shoulders.

After they had discussed the necessary logistics, River indulged her curiosity.

"If you don't mind my asking, what *is* your typical line of work?"

"Oh, it's writing. If I'm not writing, I wilt like fresh chard on the eighth day in the refrigerator. It's just not usually *marketing* writing anymore. But

I am happy to help the granddaughter of my dear friend Ella."

River could see from her expression that Vera meant her words. But it wasn't only Vera's smile that River noticed. There was an overall buoyancy to Vera that was quiet, yet unmistakable. With thanks and a promise to get Vera the photos of all of the pottery pieces in need of descriptions, River pedaled away, feeling a little lighter herself.

Chapter Eleven

THE NEXT MORNING found River in front of her closet again, wondering how important it really was to dress up for that day's meeting of the Artisans' Guild. Was the time for first impressions over yet? Deciding firmly that it was, River selected a casual pair of pants and a bright top that always made her feel cheery, partly because it was a happy color and featured embroidery, and partly because it required no ironing.

It hadn't been a great night of sleep, again. A dark cloud seemed to follow her by day and by night. She wished the cloud would get out in front and *lead* her—show her what to do. Instead, it seemed to just hover above her, pressing her down. What did God want from her in the old matter of Hannah? River used to pray about this kind of thing while working clay. Solutions and ideas just came to her then. Nothing like that had happened when she worked on the website.

As she assembled her packed lunch—tuna salad plopped on top of a bowl of baby greens—River wondered if any of the housecats in town were experiencing shortages in their regular rations because she had been eating so much canned tuna the past several weeks. *I'll eat something else after this,* she promised herself. *I'll even try some new things. Maybe that will help get my mind unstuck from this rut it's in.*

❧

The Artisans' Guild meeting was expected to be a long one that day, as the group would be discussing the Guild website, as well as planning some of the details of the AutumnFest events. The meeting room was already filling up fast and was noisy with informal conversation when River arrived, ten minutes early.

She saw Kate waving at her from across the room, and went to sit with her.

"Where's Danny?"

"He'll be here. It was one of those mornings at our house. I decided to wash the shower soap caddy in the dishwasher, but all of the dried-on bath soap that was stuck to it made suds come out all over the kitchen floor."

River was curious how the pair had determined who would cover emergency cleanup at home and who would proceed to being on time for this civic duty. And she briefly wondered which of them felt they had gotten the better end of the deal.

Crotchety Mr. Lyle seemed to have gotten out of bed on his usual side that day—whichever side that was.

"Madam chairwoman," he began, at the first moment it was appropriate for any discussion at all to come from the floor, "this whole website business is a drain on my cash register, my time, and my patience."

On the other side of the room, Mrs. Hayes, the antiquarian, nodded her head violently in agreement with Mr. Lyle, and glowered disapprovingly at Natalie, as if everything wrong in the world had been the personal doing of this mild-mannered jewelry maker elected as temporary Guild leader.

Poor Natalie, thought River. *I'll bet* she *wishes she were somewhere else cleaning up a mess right now.*

But Natalie kept her cheerful disposition as she replied to the disgruntled older man.

"Mr. Lyle, thank you for sharing your feedback with the group."

Feedback is always a gift, River thought, with a silent mental snort. She hadn't believed it when she had heard it in her college business communication class, and she didn't believe it now.

"I hope," Natalie continued, as Mr. Lyle directed a smoldering glare somewhere into the middle space of the air and folded his arms high over his narrow chest, "that your sacrifice now will pay off very well in the future, and I believe that it will, because that is why we are all doing these marketing activities, after all."

She smiled encouragingly at him. In response, Mr. Lyle wrinkled his mouth in such a way to indicate that he didn't share her hopes even in the least measure, but that he would cease complaining about it—for now.

Just then, Danny arrived and slipped into the chair that Kate had saved for him.

"What did I miss?" he whispered to his wife.

The artist who had produced the rendition of the Valley's shops for the Guild's website home page was ready to present his work. The assembled Guild members were treated to their first look at the image of their shops, as it was projected onto one wall of the meeting room.

The artwork was a sort of caricature of the buildings, drawn in what looked like markers. It really was quite good, and River felt herself getting excited that Natalie might be right, after all—the group's hard work on the Guild's website really *could* end up paying off.

Out of the corner of her eye, River thought she saw Mrs. Hayes give a look of wonder at seeing her own antique mall portrayed in a new light. She had the fleeting thought that she wished she knew what was going through that lady's head, but then decided that was a place it might be wise to steer clear of.

Chapter Twelve

RIVER HAD BEEN so wrapped up in work that she hadn't even made time to visit her relatives. That would change tonight. Instead of cooking something new, as she had promised herself that morning, River had gladly accepted the dinner invitation from Aunt Della, who had called that afternoon.

It was a Monday, and the café was closed on Mondays, so her great-aunt and great-uncle would be free to enjoy some family time with their niece.

Around Aunt Della's kitchen table, over a simple but satisfying dinner of loaded turkey burgers, sauteed local asparagus, and cinnamon baked apples with iced coffee, the three discussed their lives.

In the course of conversation, Uncle Jim shared that he had built a turntable and some other props for taking photos of the food at the café—photos to be used on their new menu—and that he and his sister had just finished working their way through cooking and photographing all of the café's offerings.

Uncle Jim offered to lend River the turntable to use for some of her own photography of pottery for her website, and she gladly accepted. He said he had taken it back to the guest house—which, despite its name, was where he had lived as a bachelor for as long as River could remember—and promised to get it and load it in her car before she left that evening.

Later, while Jim went to get the turntable for her, River and Della went out front to look at the flowers. River had always loved hearing Della recite their names: cosmos, zinnias, hostas, coral bells, balloon flowers, gomphrena, coleus—the various names spilled over River's ears like music. Great-Aunt Della, just as Grandma Ella had, loved plants. She seemed to instinctively know what they liked and needed, and they flourished under her care. People had always said that the sisters had green thumbs.

River's next stop after dinner was the natural food market at the edge of town. She realized as soon as she got inside, however, that her shopping list was still at home on the counter. She tried to visualize the paper, to remember anything at all that was written on it, but it was no use. She would either have to drive home and get it, or just wing it and certainly not remember most of what was needed. Either way meant a repeat trip to the grocery store, so River decided to stay and do the best she could—and to start keeping her list in her phone.

As she had promised herself that morning, River didn't get tuna this time. She would try some new things. Ground lamb—that was healthy. And coconut lime chips—that sounded interesting. River went through the aisles, picking out enough vegetables, fruit, meat, and other needful items to last her the rest of the week. When she reached the register, she realized aloud that her reusable shopping bags were still out in the car.

The laid-back clerk was understanding.

"You have time to go get them if you want while I ring this up."

River gratefully went out to her car to get the bags.

❧

It wasn't hunger, but curiosity, that led River to tear open the bag of coconut lime chips as soon as she got home. *These are definitely weird,* she thought, reaching for another one. *Something like shocking to the taste buds.* River wasn't sure whether she liked them or not.

She started a shopping list in her phone and typed *coconut lime chips* so she wouldn't forget to get more.

Chapter Thirteen

THE NEXT DAY, River sat at the little table she had put behind the counter at the pottery shop to allow her to be available to customers while she worked at her laptop. She searched for websites of other custom pottery stores to see what, if anything, she might have left out when planning her own site.

On the lined notepad next to her computer, she made some notes. She didn't know how to do everything that she wanted to include on her website, but with all the tutorials and YouTube videos and help forums in the world, she was sure she could figure it out. Knowing that Vera would be writing the product descriptions had taken a weight off her mind, and River now felt like she could deal with the rest.

She was actually even looking forward to doing the photography. River had always had a pretty good eye for photo composition, and thought it would be fun to use the turntable to capture the best angle of each piece of Grandma's pottery—she might even show various angles, or even a video of the entire 360 view. She would work on it a little each day, she told herself, and get all the product images done this week. It felt good to have a plan.

~

When River arrived home that evening and put down her bag on the chair inside the back door, she stopped a moment to look around.

Now that she felt like she could finally take a breath, River noticed she needed to spend some time making her house *homier*. Being in Aunt Della's cozy home the night before had reminded her of all the little things she had planned to do when she moved into Grandma's house, but hadn't taken the time for yet. Well, now she would.

When her family had cleared this house a few years ago after Grandma Ella's death, they had left only the furniture and basic items River would need. Most of her grandma's personal things that had been kept—including her collection of signs—were in storage at her parents' house. Now that River was living here, it was time for her to add her own touches to the house—*her* house.

She would begin at the front. At some point, someone had painted over what she was sure was a solid wood front door. River wanted to set the woodgrain free again. A stained wood door would be the perfect backdrop for decorations in every season.

There wouldn't be time to start on the actual door tonight, but she could begin gathering supplies. She wanted to use a nontoxic paint remover and stain she'd heard about.

She fished her car keys and her wallet out of her bag and headed out to the Valley's hardware store.

As she walked out to her car, Emerald zoomed up beside her.

"Hey, little bird," said River. "What are you up to?"

The tiny hummingbird flew a sharp zigzag and stopped again, hanging a few feet further away, still peering at her.

Then he jetted over to her neighbor's yard and into a tree.

❧

River's father had always said *A job well begun is a job half done.* And, in River's experience, gathering the supplies for a job was about half the work of the project. So, as she finished eating dinner that evening, River decided her reward for a job well begun would be some reading time in her hammock after dinner.

She went to the garage where she had tucked the pieces of the hammock frame on the day she'd moved in. She took them to the back yard and pushed them together one at a time until a complete frame emerged.

On a second trip to the garage, she scoured the shelves and workbench for the small box she knew contained the hammock. Finding it, she freed the silken nest from its storage box and proceeded to hook it firmly to the frame.

She had had the newest book from one of her favorite authors for weeks now, and hadn't even had time to open it. That would change right now. She would go inside, fix a glass of lemonade as she had seen Vera do, and settle down to begin reading.

With all of the preliminaries out of the way, River set down her glass on a little table, lowered herself into the hammock, kicked off her sandals, and opened the book.

As if on cue, she found herself in the eye of a hurricane of gnats.

Where had those come from? They hadn't been there while she was setting up the hammock.

She considered moving the hammock to another part of the yard, but then realized how late it was. The long days of summer could make 9 p.m. look like 7 p.m.

She sighed. She knew she needed her sleep. Her reward would have to wait.

❧

That week River worked her way through photographing the entire inventory of Grandma's pottery at the shop. As she did, she could feel her excitement rising. This was really her shop now, and she could—she *would*—really make a life here.

While handling the various pieces to photograph them, ideas began to come to River for new pieces she could create. She cast a glance at the empty wheel. *Now's not a good time for that,* she told herself. *But I'll get back to the wheel just as soon as this website is ready. After all, I want this business to thrive and be successful.*

Chapter Fourteen

DURING ONE OF River's brief pop-ins to the woodworking shop that week, Kate mentioned a nearby farmers market that she planned to visit that weekend, and asked if River would like to go.

"It's kind of half fresh produce, half flea market," said Kate. "I plan to go early, so we'd be back in plenty of time for you to open your shop on Saturday morning, if you're interested."

It really sounded like fun. River accepted the invitation.

⁂

When Saturday morning came, the weather was perfect for the farmers market outing. It hadn't had a chance to get too hot yet.

River visited a booth with handmade wreaths of every kind, and found one that looked just right for her front door. She also picked up some locally grown cucumbers, a jar of cultured vegetables, and an adorable painted throw pillow with a hummingbird on it.

Kate had her arms and hands similarly laden with wares, when they both stopped at a soapmaker's booth on their way back to Kate's car. In addition to exotic-smelling bars of toxin-free bath soap, the maker's display also included lip balm in little cardboard tubes, and almost every other body care product imaginable.

River thought of the shopping list in her phone, and knew that she actually needed some of the items on offer—and that she'd like to support a local maker. So, placing the throw pillow between her knees, resting the wreath on top of her feet, and transferring her bag of food items to hang from the crook of her left arm, River used her free right arm to shop, while Kate did much the same.

Then, carrying all their purchases—seemingly as awkwardly as possible—the two women talked and laughed as they left the farmers market, already discussing how soon they might return.

During the drive back to town, River and Kate made plans to meet at the café for dinner one day before the next Guild meeting. Everyone was supposed to bring ideas to that meeting for some of the AutumnFest events, and Kate said she thought it would be fun to brainstorm together over dinner—with Danny included. Kate said the change of location and a shared meal might help fuel their creativity. And, even if it didn't, they would still have a good time.

It was at times like these that River almost forgot her problems—her leaky memory, and her absolute lack of knowing what to do with the renewed feeling of heaviness at having hurt Hannah years ago.

There were some things she couldn't change, River thought, philosophically. Life went on. She would just have to carry these things the best she could—even if it seemed at times as if she were trundling along awkwardly through life with a metaphorical giant wreath over one arm and a throw pillow under the other one, while trying to carry on with the rest of her business. She supposed that's why problems were called burdens.

Chapter Fifteen

THAT EVENING, AFTER a full day at the shop and a simple dinner that included some of the farmers market produce, River rolled the old push reel mower out of the garage and set out cutting the grass. Her dad had offered to buy her a power mower, but River had wanted to keep the antique. She remembered being enthralled as a child with its workings, and she remained only slightly less enthralled by it now. She liked the relative quiet of the simple machine, and the way the grass clippings cascaded in sprays of disorganized little waves from behind the blades as she pushed the contraption around the back yard, and then the front.

River noticed a different hummingbird than the one she usually saw, as it visited some blooms in the backyard. This one appeared smaller than Emerald. She would have to think of a good name for this newly discovered pet of hers.

While mowing the front yard, River discovered that Sara had made a start on the mailbox mural revisions, and wondered when she had found time to do that. It was fun to see a start made to the project. She thought of the Scripture about the Lord rejoicing to see the work begin.

I do, too, thought River.

It was one of her favorite parts of making pottery: the beginning. In some ways, unformed clay was as far as possible from what it would be when it was complete. But when an idea arose in her mind, unformed clay was the very thing that would allow her to share that idea with the world.

River thought it was generous of God to share creativity with his creatures. *Not only do we get to* be *his creation*, she thought; *we also get to* participate *in it*. Sometimes River felt that was when she was closest to God: when she was creating.

It had been a good day. And a long one. River eyed the hammock frame and decided to take another shot at reading her book. After a quick shower, she retrieved the silk hammock from its basket inside the back door, carried it outside, and connected it to the frame. She placed herself in its smooth cradle. But instead of reading as she had hoped, she found that the fresh air and exercise at both ends of the day had prepared her for sleep. She made it only a few paragraphs before her eyes closed and the book tilted downward. When she awoke a few minutes later, she took herself inside the house and put herself to bed, where sleep found her again.

Chapter Sixteen

RIVER DIDN'T BOTHER with routine the next morning.

Instead, she carried the new wreath outside to see how it would look on the front door. She stood in her pajamas in the freshly mown yard, looking at the wreath, drinking in its colors and textures and design. She would work on stripping the door soon. She couldn't wait to see the beautiful wood she was sure was hidden under that paint.

Then she carried the new throw pillow around inside the house, moving it from the couch to a chair to her bed, trying to decide where the painted hummingbird should alight. It looked good everywhere she put it.

After a few minutes of that, her stomach requested food, so she left the pillow on the chair and went in search of breakfast. If she were going to be on time for church, she would have to get a move on.

A trip to the market was on River's agenda for the afternoon. She had invited her aunt and uncle over for a cookout Monday night, and she needed to get the food for that, as well as the rest of her supplies for the week.

After lunch, River stood at her kitchen counter and worked on the shopping list. This time, it would be in her phone. Referring to some recipes that she planned to make that week, she added their ingredients to her list, including a few unfamiliar spices and other items that she didn't have on hand. Then she did a visual inspection of staples on shelves and in cupboards, to remind herself of anything else that needed to be put on the list to be purchased that day. The list grew, until finally River felt satisfied that it was ready for action.

She had just pulled her little car into a spot in the parking lot of the market and reached for her bag when River realized that her phone—and her robust shopping list—wasn't in her bag. Or anywhere in her car.

It was still at home on the counter.

Chapter Seventeen

AS IT HAPPENED, there was a third guest for the Monday night cookout in River's backyard.

Sara had been at River's house early that morning working on a layer of the mailbox mural when River had left for the pottery shop, and had mentioned that she planned to work on the mural again that evening. On a sudden impulse, River had invited her to join them for dinner, and Sara had accepted.

While Uncle Jim got the grill started in the backyard, and Sara wrapped up her brushes and paint and stored them in the caddy in her car out front, River and Aunt Della stood in River's kitchen, loading wooden kebab sticks with vegetables and marinated meat.

"I would have done this earlier," said River, "but the recipe said to soak the wooden sticks for 20 minutes beforehand, and I figured that meant immediately beforehand, so that's what I did."

Della agreed that that sounded best, and assured River that she didn't mind helping.

After a few moments of quiet, Della gave a low laugh, and commented softly to River, "Did you notice the look on my brother's face when he saw Sara here?"

River had noticed, and had wondered about it, but hadn't said anything.

"Do they know each other?" River asked, in a soft tone to match her great-aunt's.

"We all went to school together, and I think they were in the same class," said Della, and then heard the front door opening, so abruptly ended her explanation there.

When Sara asked what she could do to help, River gave a quick glance at her aunt before replying, "Well, you could take these kebabs out to Uncle Jim and ask him to put them on the grill."

River and Aunt Della soon followed, carrying canning jars of lemonade and sun tea, and then a large bowl of salad and a stack of plates and utensils.

The four sat around the patio table and fell easily into comfortable conversation.

River laughed. "You're going to have to avert your eyes from Grandma's garden—my garden—this summer. Gardening is just not in my schedule right now with everything else that's going on. But hopefully next year I can give it the attention it needs."

Just then, Emerald and the other hummingbird River had seen while she was mowing both came to inspect a nearby bloom in the untamed garden—and, it seemed, to put on a pre-dinner show.

The smaller bird and Emerald both fanned out their tail feathers—and then appeared to stand upright in the air and butt chests! They began rushing at each other, apparently over grazing rights to the bloom they had both inspected. They were either oblivious to their human onlookers or just didn't care about collateral damage, because their flight paths grew recklessly close to their audience.

It almost seemed that the two birds were coming close on purpose, as if to add the humans to their claim of territory. The smaller hummingbird, which River had decided to call

Simon, suddenly rushed at Sara's head, before turning and darting at Jim's head. River just stared, while Della and Sara and Jim succumbed to gales of laughter at the bird's silliness, apparently feeling themselves safe in the belief that no hummingbird ever had—or ever would—miscalculate his flight trajectory in such a way as to impale a person's head. They laughed so hard that the two hummingbirds stopped fighting to hang in midair and stare at them.

River had never seen this kind of behavior from the beautiful little creatures, and wondered if the reaction of her elders' generation was more—or less—in line with the actual level of threat the tiny birds' pointy beaks posed. She had considered the hummingbirds her pets. But were they actually more like wild beasts than the delicate flying jewels she had imagined them to be? Should she wear protective eyewear when she went near flowers?

But in the next moment, River's attention was diverted by another surprising sight. On the grill, the carefully soaked wooden kebab sticks had caught on fire. The neat row of tiny skewers bearing their food was now a tidy line of four-inch-high flames. In an uncalculated move, River grabbed a full jar of sun tea and doused the flames with it.

A good time was had by all.

Chapter Eighteen

RIVER HAD SENT an email to Vera letting her know when all of the product photography was complete. There were so many files that they had agreed that Vera would stop by the shop to pick up a USB flash drive of the photos.

When Vera arrived the next day, River was huddled over her laptop at the table behind the counter, examining the various options of contact forms she could add to her site.

"I've nearly forgotten how I used to spend my time before I started making this website," River observed to Vera with a smile.

"There are seasons to things," Vera replied thoughtfully. "When it's time, you will remember."

Vera had brought a gift for River, which she said was a business-warming gift. It was a beautifully hand-lettered, framed sign that read:

WE ARE THE CLAY, AND YOU OUR POTTER. ISAIAH 64:8.

"Vera, this is amazing," said River, appreciatively gazing at the bold lettering and allowing the words into her mind. And then, looking at the older woman, "Thank you."

"You're most welcome, River."

Just then, that rare bird, the weekday customer, was spotted entering the shop. Vera moved to one side to allow River to greet the woman.

River handed Vera the USB drive containing the photos, and Vera said she would email an update in a few days, before giving a smile and making a graceful exit.

Chapter Nineteen

RIVER HAD PROMISED herself some reading time in the hammock. It was easier to read outside in a hammock than to try to relax indoors, where the call of things like laundry and dirty dishes could more easily reach one's ears. But an oppressive period of heat and humidity—a hallmark of southern Indiana summers—made that idea an impractical one.

Her book, however, called even more loudly than her household tasks. So, the next night, she set aside the hummingbird pillow, settled into her chair, and let herself be carried into the fictional story.

Later that night, head on her bed pillow, River wondered how an author might write the story of her and Hannah from this point on. River didn't have a clue. She didn't know anything about Hannah or her life now. She didn't know if

Hannah even thought about that part of their shared past that River had now remembered.

God, River prayed, *what kind of story are you wanting to write here? Is there another chapter you want to add to the story of Hannah and me? Or do you just want to edit a story that's already been written? Is that even possible?*

It had been sort of a rhetorical prayer, and so River was surprised to hear an answer in that silent inner voice—the unmistakable impression of words—words she knew were from God.

Write to her.

And say what?, River wondered. *And send the letter where?*

But she heard no answer.

Chapter Twenty

THE NEXT MORNING, River decided that the first step in writing to Hannah was to find out if she could even get an address for her. She didn't know if Hannah's last name had changed, or where she lived, but she had to start somewhere.

She did an online search that had way too many results, none of which looked promising, but that also brought up the obituary of Hannah's father. In it, in the list of family members surviving the deceased, was the name of Hannah's brother, Neil. When River searched for Neil's full name, she found an article about him receiving a business promotion at a company in the town where River had visited Hannah's family.

Bingo. She could write to Neil at his work address. In fact, she saw that she could email him through his company website.

Remembering the saying that delayed obedience was the same as disobedience, River decided to write to Neil that morning asking for Hannah's address.

Chapter Twenty-One

WHEN THE EVENING came to meet Kate and Danny at the café for dinner and AutumnFest brainstorming, River arrived early so she could have a quick visit with Aunt Della and Uncle Jim. River had also brought the turntable to return to Uncle Jim.

"That worked great!" she exclaimed, handing the contraption over to her great-uncle. "Thank you!"

"Well, good," he said, a pleased expression spreading over his weathered face. "I'm glad it was useful."

As Della walked by them with a customer's change, she leaned over to where the two were talking and gave River a quick hug.

"Hello, sweetie," she said. "I'll be back in a minute."

When Della returned, River and Jim were discussing what tools she might borrow from him in order to open a coconut.

"What are you doing with a coconut?" asked Della.

"Nothing, yet," admitted River. "But I saw some at the natural food market last weekend, and I've always wanted to try fresh coconut milk. And, as Grandma always said, there's no time like the present. I just don't want to accidentally lose a hand in the process."

Della laughed.

"No, that might be bad for business."

"Well, I've looked at some different videos online," River explained, "and I think I can use a screwdriver and a rubber mallet, except I don't have a rubber mallet."

"I can get you set up there," said Jim. "In fact, I'll go get one for you right now."

As Jim was walking out, he met a party of three entering the café and held the door open for them. It was Kate and Danny—and Sara.

"Hello, hello, all," he said, in his friendly way. "Sara, I'll be right back as soon as I get a rubber mallet for River. And then we will head out." His expansive smile was returned with an equally broad smile from Sara.

River directed a quizzical look toward her great-aunt, who replied by greeting the three, "Hello! Danny and Kate, River told us you'd be joining her here for dinner tonight. We're glad you're here. And Sara, it's so nice to see you, too; can I get you anything to drink before you and Jim leave?"

River had to remind herself to close her mouth and find her manners, which she did, just in time. She wasn't sure what surprised her more: the idea of her longtime-bachelor great-uncle apparently going on a date, or the idea of its being with Sara, a woman who'd lived practically under his nose for decades.

At the café, River, Kate, and Danny spent the rest of the evening eating, laughing, and saying any AutumnFest idea that came into their heads, no matter how farfetched it seemed. Danny carried in his shirt pocket the small carpenter's notepad and pencil that lived there most of the time, and River and Kate had both brought lined notepads and two ink pens each. With the three of them so well-armed, it was unlikely that any truly good idea spotted had a chance of avoiding capture.

Della had only a few other customers in the café that night, mostly Valley locals who had dropped in for the dinner special or just a cup of coffee. After all of the other diners had left, Della sat down with the three brainstormers, and they all enjoyed each other's company.

❧

At home later that night, River thought about what a good time they had had, despite how aware they all were of how much their livelihoods depended on the success of planning and carrying out events like AutumnFest. She had been feeling the pressure for weeks. But she was glad to know that there could also be fun in the process. *Don't muzzle an ox as he treads out the grain*, she thought.

Her phone made a noise and she picked it up to find a text from her brother.

Nick: Hey, Riv. What's up?
River: Big Guild meeting tomorrow to plan AutumnFest. How are you?
Nick: I'm good. Classes are good. Would be nice to get there for that.
River: Can you come? Will your classes be over?
Nick: Not yet, so not sure. I'll have to check.
River: Ok. Would be cool. Guess who had a date tonight?

River wondered, as she typed the last line, whether this was gossip. She sat with the sentence for a moment before hitting send, considering her heart and her motives. She was happy for Uncle Jim. This was good news. And Nick would be happy for his great-uncle, too.

Nick: Who's the guy??
River: No, not me. Uncle Jim had a date.
Nick: Seriously?!?
River: Yes. With a painter here. Neat lady.
Nick: Wow. Unexpected.
River: They both looked really happy.
Nick: Awesome. Good to hear.

Chapter Twenty-Two

THERE WAS A buzz of energy in the packed room the next afternoon at the Guild meeting. Some were eager to share their ideas for AutumnFest. Others were eager to hear ideas better than the ones they had brought.

As she sat in her now-usual spot next to Kate, River pulled her notepad out of her bag, and, in doing so, accidentally launched her two ink pens into the air. They landed and slid across the slick tile floor. Just as she was returning to her seat from retrieving them, Natalie called the meeting to order.

In addition to flying ink pens, River had also brought a glass bottle of her now-favorite homemade lemonade with her. She carefully pulled it from her bag and took a drink, all the while focusing her attention on Natalie. Their leader was thanking everyone for the time she knew they had spent in coming up with the ideas that would be shared today, and setting a positive tone of the kind generally thought to be conducive to group creativity.

Natalie then asked for people to begin sharing their ideas. She announced that Alicia—an energetic woman wearing a t-shirt that read GET NUTTY—would write them down on the large white board set up for that purpose. River checked her notes. Alicia was the owner of a nut shop. *That explains the shirt*, she thought.

Seemingly entirely immune to the positive tone Natalie had so carefully created for the meeting, Mr. Lyle took this earliest opportunity to speak from his heart.

He complained about how much time this meeting was going to take away from his work, and concluded with an emphatic, "Those brooms don't make themselves," that struck River's funny bone exactly in its tickle spot. She instantly and involuntarily envisioned the inside of Mr. Lyle's shop in his absence, with its entire company of broom handles and broom heads—and even individual straws—dancing and singing and carrying out all kinds of activities in animated-musical style, always careful not to indicate any sort of progress to their master on his return.

River had not meant to laugh. And, actually, she hadn't laughed. It had been more of a snort. Since she had just taken another drink of her lemonade, her faux pas was convincingly covered by a very real round of coughing and choking, genuine enough to draw a look of concern from Kate. Although her choking had more than disguised the reaction that had started it all, River considered it a close call.

Really, she thought. *If I am going to deal with the public on a regular basis—and especially with other shop owners in this community—I am going to have to develop some more composure.*

She looked at Natalie, patiently enduring the barrage of words from Mr. Lyle, all the while wearing a pleasant expression. River gazed more intently at Natalie to try to determine whether she was merely tolerating him politely, or if her bearing arose from some deeper, rarer treasure.

When Mr. Lyle had finished his tirade and Natalie had responded with kindness, River thought she saw Natalie subtly shift her gaze to

Mrs. Hayes, owner of the antique mall, to see if that lady would be adding her own complaints to the pile begun by Mr. Lyle. But Mrs. Hayes had a faraway look in her eyes as if she were already enjoying AutumnFest, or at least anticipating it with pleasure.

And as the rest of the meeting unfolded, it was that spirit, and not the one Mr. Lyle had fed, that prevailed.

Sara, the painter, offered her idea of creating an artsy, hand-drawn map of the town. She suggested a similar style to that of the drawing on the Guild's website. The map would serve as a directory of each participating shop, and paper copies of the maps could be available for visitors to pick up at each shop.

"We could also offer the map as a download on the guild website and our individual business websites," said Danny.

Alicia took a break from writing on the whiteboard long enough to add her own suggestion that they have a horse-drawn carriage decorated like a pumpkin available for hired rides. She turned back to the board to record the idea, just in time to miss the few raised eyebrows and glances exchanged here and there, as other business owners wondered where they would get a horse, a carriage, and a driver—but also considered how much they might truly like to see the sight for themselves, and perhaps right in front of their own shops.

Natalie thought that setting up creative selfie photo stations around the Valley and generating some hashtags would be a good way to encourage social media exposure.

Matt, a second-generation basket maker and self-confessed social media addict, enthusiastically agreed and shared several other ideas for social media promotion.

River then floated her concept of having giveaways each day during the event. Each shop owner could donate items from their own inventory to be used as door prizes, she said. As she spoke, River tried to gauge the reactions of the other business owners to the idea of parting with their wares, and was relieved that it seemed to be positive. She took a careful sip of her lemonade to indicate that she was finished speaking, and perhaps also to reinforce an image of herself as competent to swallow.

There was no lull in conversation, as, one after another, the other shop owners added their own brainchildren to the growing list of ideas that Alicia scribbled nearly nonstop on the whiteboard with a juicy black marker, newly purchased for the occasion.

Kate said that she had just taken a webinar about building a business email list, and she thought the Guild as a whole could benefit from starting an email list to help promote future events. She suggested that people could subscribe at the Guild's website.

Anna, the herbalist, suggested decorating all of the shop entrances with matching tubs of colorful fall plants.

The owner of the knittery, a petite woman named Dora Fusselman, added in her quiet but clear voice that she had thought, if the budget permitted, perhaps they could even have themed banners made for the lampposts along the sidewalk.

There was a general murmur of approval as the concept was duly noted on the whiteboard, which was now so full that Alicia had to stoop over and write at a very awkward angle in the space remaining at the bottom. It seemed that the meeting would have to end soon, because there wasn't much room left in which to record any more ideas.

When Mrs. Hayes proposed a sort of progressive open house, with various appetizers or hot drinks served at each shop, Alicia had paused for a moment from her scribe duties to stretch her spine and glance around the room.

From the expressions of those gathered, it seemed as if this idea, too, would soon become an AutumnFest tradition in the Valley of Artisans.

On her bike ride home after the Guild meeting, River made a detour to the natural food market, just to buy a coconut.

At home in her tidy kitchen, she pulled the coconut out of her bag and applied a screwdriver and the borrowed rubber mallet to open it. She held up the orb in her uninjured hands, and watched with satisfaction as the watery liquid streamed from the coconut into a bowl.

And then, holding the bowl with both hands as a little child would hold a cup, River stood in the kitchen and drank it all.

Chapter Twenty-Three

A FEW DAYS later, in much the same way that hummingbirds announce their arrival by suddenly appearing, River realized that her long uphill trudge with her website was nearly complete.

She had figured out all of the issues on her list, taken all of the photos of her inventory, and received all of the product descriptions Vera had written for her. All that was left to do was upload the photos and input the descriptions and prices of each of Grandma's pieces.

She even had everything ready that she needed to submit to the organizer of the Guild's festival website.

It was a good feeling. Like coming up from underneath a tangle of seaweed in murky water, and taking a breath of the air.

River felt like celebrating. And she would have her opportunity. The Artisans' Guild was hosting a progressive open house after hours that weekend to give the shop owners a chance to visit each other's shops before the festival began, and see the progress that had been made so far.

When Saturday came, River opened her shop at the usual time and was surprised to see an unfamiliar delivery truck pull up out front just a few minutes later.

As she watched, a large bouquet of raspberry colored calla lilies in a sturdy white vase walked through her door, with a blue uniform jacket behind it and two blue uniformed legs below.

The clove-like scent of the lilies pervaded the air around her, as River thanked the delivery person and opened the card.

"Congrats on the new venture. Love, Nick." Her brother was truly happy for her new life here, River thought. She knew her entire family was. As busy as they all were with their own lives, each one had supported her in their own unique ways, and for that she was grateful.

River placed the arrangement on the counter, to be enjoyed by her customers as well as everyone who would visit during that night's open house.

The hours slipped by quickly that day, as River helped the few customers who came in, interspersed with uploading the last of the website photos, descriptions, and prices. At lunch and dinner time, she ate at her small worktable without taking a break, and finally completed her website.

She had crossed the finish line the way many personal marathons finish: with no fanfare other than a quiet sigh of relief.

River saw she had just enough time to check her email before she needed to switch gears for the open house.

At first, she didn't recognize the name of the sender of one of her messages, Neil. She clicked on the message with curiosity, and began reading.

It was from Hannah's brother, whom she had emailed at work. His note was short but kind. He hoped that she and her family were doing well. And he had included Hannah's address.

There it was, right in front of her. Her last reason, or excuse, for not contacting Hannah had just been obliterated. *Well*, thought River. *Now I will write to her.*

Just then, River saw Uncle Jim's car pull up in front of her shop, and she closed her email and went out to meet him. Aunt Della had made the finger food for River to serve at tonight's event, and Uncle Jim was dropping it off. As she and her great-uncle took her two boxes of appetizers from the trunk of the car, she noticed two more boxes of food on the back seat.

"Those boxes in the back seat aren't mine, are they?" asked River.

River thought she saw some pink creep up the sides of Jim's neck as he replied.

"No, those are for Sara's open house. I'm going to stay there and help her this evening."

River gave a businesslike nod of approval. After all, if the business owners were going to see each other's shops, it stood to reason that someone would need to remain at their shops while they did so.

She had actually thought about asking Vera to come and help her tonight with her own open house. She was sure Vera, having been her grandma's best friend, must have spent a lot of time at the pottery shop. But then she had thought better of it.

Kate had offered to come by at the start of the open house and sit in at the pottery shop while River made a quick round of the other open houses. Then Kate and Danny would take turns watching their own store, so they could each tour the other shops.

When the set time for the open house arrived, Kate appeared, as promised, in the doorway of River's shop.

"Thank you so much for doing this," said River. "I won't take long."

"Take your time," said Kate graciously. "I haven't had a chance to browse in here and this will be the perfect opportunity."

River enjoyed her quick tour. She didn't even chide herself for not being able to remember owners' names. Her notes wouldn't have helped tonight: many of the Guild members weren't even in their own stores, as they had arranged shop-sitters so they could enjoy the event. River just gave her best warm smile and hello to each one she saw and hoped that genuine friendliness would cover for her remaining neurocognitive glitches.

River walked briskly back to her own shop, enjoying the fresh feeling of fall in the mildly cool air. It wouldn't be long now, she thought, until cool turned to chilly. But River loved these early mellow days of the new season.

Her musings were cut short by her arrival at the familiar door. She thanked Kate for covering for her, and then decided to try her own appetizers.

Vera was the next guest to enter after River's return.

"This is only the second time I've been in here since Ella died," said Vera, smiling appreciatively as she looked around the clean, well-lit pottery shop. "It is good to be here."

A warm feeling of compassion for Vera washed over River. Of course, River thought, Vera must still be missing her best friend.

River said she thought it would be nice, if Vera had time, for Vera to sit a while and visit, and Vera accepted. River went to the back room to bring out a chair for her guest.

When River got back to the front, Vera was walking slowly through the display aisles, looking at the pottery pieces for sale.

"Ella's work is beautiful," she said simply. "I can't wait to see yours."

Chapter Twenty-Four

LATER THAT NIGHT, with a plate of some sliced radishes and hummus left over from the open house, River flipped open her laptop on her kitchen table at home.

She would handwrite the note to mail to Hannah, but she would have to compose it electronically first. There wouldn't be enough stationery in the world for all of the drafts she would go through if she tried to compose this letter on paper instead of copying her already-typed note onto a page.

Quiet fell over her house as River went deep into a place in her mind, and her heart, to try to find what she needed to say.

In the end, her words seemed to come from neither of those places, but from the Spirit whom she had asked for guidance. After all, she thought, it had been his idea for her to contact Hannah in the first place, so, apparently, he knew what this was all about.

She still didn't know what the point was of bringing up a pain so old that there seemed no reason to think about it. Except that she knew, somehow, it was God who wanted to do something here.

So, she trusted him to guide her thoughts and her words. And he did. And then she copied those words onto some stationery with a picture of birds at the top. And she placed a stamp on the envelope addressed to Hannah, and walked outside in the dark to place it in her mailbox, hearing only the soft thwack, thwack of her flip flops in the night air as she returned to the house.

And then she slept.

Chapter Twenty-Five

THE FOLLOWING MONDAY morning was sunny and clear when River pulled the leather sandal keychain out of her bag to open the pottery shop.

It was that first week signaling autumn in Indiana, when the temperature had begun to play with really dropping. Between early morning and late afternoon, it could warm up 40 degrees. River found that long pants and a sweatshirt, plus a hat, scarf and gloves could be required in the morning, while short pants and a short-sleeved shirt and sandals were needed for comfort by afternoon.

River didn't mind. The transition was just another reminder of how change was built in to life. Seeds fell, were watered, and grew. Plants sprouted, and matured, and produced whatever they were designed to create, and then they returned to the ground.

She actually found the crisp morning air invigorating, and noticed herself humming—not something she usually did—as she opened her laptop on the small worktable behind the counter.

River had given herself a complete break from email on Sunday while she immersed herself in a good book. This was the time of year when several of her favorite authors were all coming out with new books at nearly the same time, and for a reader like River, it was a bonanza. The hummingbird pillow had proved to be a comfortable ally to her reading, and she had brewed herself a cup of cocoa in her new French press. The cocoa beans and the press had been a thoughtful gift from her parents to congratulate her on her reopening of the pottery shop.

River quickly scanned the unread emails—she liked to know what the pottery supply companies were up to and watch for sales on glazes and other supplies. But she always checked emails from people she knew first.

This morning, there was an email waiting for her with a file attached. It was the new logo she had commissioned for her shop. Grandma Ella had never really had a logo for the shop—or a name for it, other than *Pottery Shop*—something River first became acutely aware of when she was creating her website. And so, River had come up with some new name ideas. She had contacted a friend of hers who was a freelance graphic artist, and now, here were three logo options for River to consider.

River excitedly opened the files. Each of the options was beautiful. They were exactly what she had asked for.

And yet, none of them felt right.

And River didn't know why.

Chapter Twenty-Six

THE JINGLE OF the bell on the shop door diverted River's attention from her computer. It was Kate, bringing River two of the pumpkin spice muffins she had made the night before from a new almond-flour recipe she had found.

"I had two of them for breakfast," Kate giggled. "Once Danny tries them, between the two of us, the whole batch will probably be gone by the end of the day, so I figured I'd better bring yours over now."

Kate handed River the treats, which she had wrapped in some waxed paper.

"Oh, yum. Thank you! Do you mind if I go ahead and have one?" River asked. "I think it's late enough that I can call it an early lunch."

Kate laughed.

"You go right ahead," said Kate. "I was wondering if you want to go to the farmers market again sometime? I can't go this Saturday, but I was thinking about maybe the week after?"

River immediately accepted.

"Great! It'll be fun," said Kate. "Hey, did you hear the news about the B&B?"

"No, what's up?" replied River, unwrapping the waxed paper and lifting one of the muffins to its destiny.

"Well, the Bowers—Natalie's parents—opened it about 20 years ago, but they'd been talking for a while about hanging it up soon, with business being so slow. I don't know what they were going to do with that huge old house. But now, Natalie's got them so excited about all of the stuff the town is doing to build tourism back up, that they've decided to keep it open and get involved with the Guild's new promotions. I think that is going to be great for the rest of us. After all, it's pretty hard for people to consider the Valley as a tourist destination if there's no place to lay their heads."

"Wow, that's great to hear," said River. "And so true about helping tourism.

"Maybe you can give them this muffin recipe," she added. "This is amazing."

"Thanks," said Kate. "Every fall I think I could eat pumpkin every day for the rest of my life, and then December comes along and I get distracted by peppermint and chocolate."

They laughed.

"Yeah, I can see how that could be a distraction," said River.

"Well, I'd better get back to the shop. I hope you have a million customers today!"

River smiled at Kate's benevolent silliness.

"And I hope you have a million, too."

River thanked Kate again for the sweet surprise, and then, as her friend closed the door behind her, turned back to her computer to finish getting caught up from the weekend.

River logged into the website to check on any orders she might have received online and was surprised—and excited—to see that she had made several large sales on the website.

From the look of things, she would need to get busy packing and shipping pottery. She had thought she was prepared to ship orders, but as she glanced through the orders, it quickly became apparent that she was going to need even more shipping supplies—and soon.

Chapter Twenty-Seven

RIVER SPENT MOST of the day pulling items off the shelves and filling the flurry of internet orders from the weekend.

She focused intently on her tasks, even turning off the background music in the shop so she could give her full concentration to the orders. Now wasn't the time for mistakes.

She had printed all of the packing slips and shipping labels and laid them on a worktable in the back room. She pulled all of the items needed for a single order, wrapped the pottery in protective material, put it into a shipping box, and labeled the box, before moving it to a stack in the corner, ready for pickup, and starting on the next order. She'd rearrange the display shelves later.

As the day wore on, and River continued to remove more items from the shelves than she had ever expected to sell so soon, a thought hit her. These were Grandma Ella's pieces that were selling so well. Would River's own designs sell half as well when she started making them... which she hadn't yet? Would her own work even be good enough to keep Grandma's pottery business alive?

River carried the sobering thought around for a while inside the quiet shop. Her meditation was finally interrupted by a noise from the street outside. It was a school bus groaning up the main street with a load of elementary school students. River thought school buses always sounded as if their engines were overburdened with too-heavy loads of unwilling yellow metal. Since the years when she had been a regular passenger on one of the behemoths, River had always noticed the inordinate amount of screeching noise school buses made as they lurched from stop to stop and around corners.

The bus faded from earshot, and River returned her full focus to her quiet task of picking and packing orders.

A couple of hours later, River finished filling the last order. She looked at the mound of boxes that represented so much to her: her Grandma's work; customers' appreciation of beauty and functional art; River's livelihood. It was satisfying and gratifying to see her own hard work on the website paying off so soon. River was glad.

But as she walked back into the front showroom and looked around at the skimpy selection that remained, a new question rose in her mind. Did she even have enough inventory left in the shop for the festival—or time to do anything about it, if not?

It was a valid question, but not one she was prepared to face.

Before closing time that evening, River artistically arranged the remaining inventory so that the shop would still be inviting to walk-in customers. There hadn't been any at all that day, but Mondays were usually slow. Many of the shops weren't even open on Mondays. River could understand why. However, her day had been productive. Yes, she had questions to answer and things to figure out. But not tonight.

She decided the evening's agenda would include a hot dinner and an early bedtime. She locked the front door to the shop and headed home to carry out her plans.

Chapter Twenty-Eight

THE NEXT MORNING River woke early. Not even debating whether to get up, she rose, boiled some water for tea, and sat in her chair with the hummingbird pillow as she waited for the tea to steep.

Her front windows faced the sunrise, and she watched as the pink and dark-pink inky light spread itself across the sky in a style that nothing in her pottery glazes could ever replicate. She knew, because she had tried in her own creations. The results had been interesting—beautiful, even—but nothing like a real sunset. Sunsets were God's purview—not hers.

And that is when River realized why none of the new logos for the pottery shop felt right to her. The names featured in the logos were all based on someone else's work: *Grandma's Pottery, Grandma Ella's Pottery, Ella Carter Pottery Works.* Those names spoke of the past. It had been a good past—one worth honoring. But it was still the past.

She would come up with some new name ideas that reflected the present. River felt hopeful as she got up to write herself a reminder on the notepad lying on her kitchen table and retrieve her tea, which was ready.

Chapter Twenty-Nine

IT WAS SEVERAL days later, as River was entering a few more of Grandma Ella's pottery pieces into the website for sale, that she caught the error.

A feeling of dread spread over her and her heart seemed to pause for a moment as she checked again. Yes, the error was real. All of the prices she had previously entered in the website had not been the retail selling price, but instead, she had entered her own cost for the pieces—effectively cutting out her entire profit margin on everything she had sold online so far. No wonder the items had sold so quickly—she'd unintentionally set bargain-basement prices for premium pottery.

River knew she had double checked those prices while entering them. This had happened, not because of a lack of care or lack of knowledge, but simply because of some remaining unhealed neurocognitive glitch, some unpredictable wild card. She was frustrated beyond measure. The floor seemed to give way beneath what confidence she had had that she was recovered enough to run this business. Would her brain ever be ready again?

It had failed her big time.

And not for the first time. This was similar to what had happened when she had been signing the title to the used car she had bought before moving here. River was fully aware that she was the *buyer* of the car, and she knew the meanings of the terms *buyer* and *seller*. Yet, when her hand reached to sign the title, her brain directed her to sign the line that—in that moment—it connected with her being the buyer. The only problem was that the line the brain selected actually said *seller*. Her still-healing brain had chosen to match the word *seller* with the definition of *buyer*. And it had done so confidently. There was absolutely no wavering or indecision in the moment—no indication at all that anything might be amiss. The brain confidently made the choice as it had made thousands of other choices before and after it that day. Except, this one was incorrect—and her brain didn't even realize it.

There were definitely still neurocognitive glitches like this that she had to live with at times, but she never knew when one would exhibit itself.

In the case of the car title, the error had only cost her an extra trip to the BMV, to stand in line and sign an affidavit confirming she was not the seller of the car. But in this latest event, the glitch had cost her much more.

Just as frustrating, River thought, *is that there is nothing I can even do to prevent this kind of thing from happening again. It's not as if there is a safety net I can put in place.*

Intensifying her feeling of helplessness was the knowledge that she *had* double-checked her work the day she had entered the pottery prices into the website. And that even then, her brain had stuck by its decision that *cost* meant the *sell* price—something that River knew was not the case. The part of her brain that was supposed to detect errors of this kind had also failed to rise to the occasion, not giving River even the slightest warning. The brain had thought its work was fine—when it clearly wasn't.

Making lists and keeping notes couldn't compensate for this kind of neurological challenge. It wasn't as if someone could follow her around, verifying every executive function of her brain all day long as she ran this business. That wasn't realistic. And even if it were, River couldn't afford to hire anyone at this point—and especially not after this mistake.

Now, not only was a large chunk of her inventory gone, but she hadn't even made the profit she needed to make on those sales. And it was too late to do anything about it.

One thing had to be done right away, however. She would have to immediately fix the pricing issue on every other product still for sale on her website.

Shoulders hunched toward the computer, her mouth set in a grim line, River got to work.

Chapter Thirty

THAT EVENING, RIVER'S phone rang. It was Kate.

"Hey, how are you? I missed you at the meeting today."

"What meet—oh, no. Today was the Guild meeting."

"Yeah, is everything okay?"

The frustration of that morning quickly rushed back to River at full force, as she realized that in her urgent preoccupation to correct the prices of the remaining pottery on her website that day, she had completely forgotten the Guild meeting. She thanked Kate for her concern and explained that she had been at the shop fixing a major problem with the website. Kate was kind and said she was sorry about the trouble and was glad that River was okay.

River wondered if she *was* okay. Did other people forgot to attend meetings when they were having a rough day, or was that yet one more misadventure of a brain not yet completely healed from mold illness? She knew it was no use wondering; in her case, there was no way to know which it was.

In her experience, neurological issues gave a lot of surprise gifts—and not the good kind. When she forgot to buy goat cheese, it was easy to write that off as almost normal—everyone forgets things. When she couldn't remember names or she had to make lists—that was all garden-variety stuff.

Compared to how sick she had been just a few years before, those things seemed like child's play, and she accepted them without complaint. But when her still-healing brain paraded its more unique outstanding shortcomings in a way that threatened her ability to run her business, as it had today, a dark cloud that used to be her constant companion seemed to once again close in and press down on her.

Go ahead, it seemed to say. *Try to get on with your life. But I'm still here.*

Chapter Thirty-One

RIVER WAS RESOLVED that wallowing wasn't an option for her. She couldn't change what had happened, and she was determined to just go on from here the best she could.

It was in that spirit that the next day, Saturday, she decided to work on coming up with a new name for her shop. It was time to put her own name on this business. It was, after all, hers.

Kate had brought some fresh morning glory muffins by the shop for her that morning. "These have pumpkin and zucchini and flax seed," she'd said. "They used to be Danny's favorite, but I think he's going over to the pumpkin spice muffin side now. Let me know what you think."

And so, fueled by matcha tea and a still-warm muffin, River sat down at the little table behind the counter with her laptop, and began typing out some ideas for names for her shop.

River Carter Clay Works
River Carter Pottery
Pottery by River Carter
R. Carter, Potter

River wasn't wild about the last two, but decided to go ahead and email all of them to the graphic artist and see what she came up with.

Like an animal print shirt by itself on a hanger, River thought, there were some things one couldn't make a decision about until one saw it in context.

⁂

That evening, River closed the shop a few minutes early so that she could catch Natalie still in her jewelry shop. She wanted to apologize in person for missing the Guild meeting and let Natalie know that she was totally committed to doing her part for AutumnFest.

Natalie was so gracious that River needn't have been concerned on that score. Natalie updated River on the ideas that had been approved, including flower barrels. Everyone was being asked to clear a space on both sides of their shop entrances for the barrels, which would be delivered within the next week.

"That's no problem," said River, "I don't have any sidewalk displays or signs. Oh, and speaking of signs, I'm working on a new name and logo for my shop. I hope that won't cause an issue for the Festival materials."

"Ooh! That's exciting!" enthused the jewelry-maker. "Good for you, putting your own signature on it. And that should be an easy swap-out on the Guild website. As long as we have the new name and logo before the maps are printed, I don't see any issues with it."

River promised to get the logo files to Natalie as soon as a decision was made.

"My parents are actually thinking of renaming their B&B, too, but they have no idea what to call it," laughed Natalie.

So, the bed-and-breakfast was staying in business, thought River. This was a confirmation of good news.

"I feel for them," River said, with both seriousness and a smile.

"I told them I could think of reasons for and against renaming it," Natalie explained, "but in the end, it's their B&B and their decision."

"What's it called now?" asked River.

"The sign out front has always just said B&B, and that's what our family and everyone else has always called it," said Natalie. "To be honest, I don't even know if it has a different legal name."

River nodded. "That sounds like the café. I guess maybe when most of these businesses were started, it was the style to just say exactly what they were, and leave it at that."

Natalie laughed. "Probably so," she agreed, good-naturedly.

The beaded and bejeweled clock on the wall of Natalie's shop indicated that it was time for closing. River thanked Natalie again for her understanding, and wished her a relaxing weekend. Then she walked back to her shop to collect her bike, and pedaled home in the comfortable early fall air.

⁂

That evening, the prospect of a day without work the next day—Sunday—lured River into what she had come to think of as her reading chair.

The stack of unread books on the little table next to her chair bore witness to the chair's function, but its lips were sealed regarding how much reading was actually being done. But, as any avid reader can attest, River knew, a growing to-be-read stack is *sometimes* actually proportional to how much the person *is* reading. Reading was kind of like creativity: It tended to generate more reading.

That was fine with her. She could use an evening of being transported somewhere else in her imagination, while ensconced in her chair, snug in her house.

Chapter Thirty-Two

THE FOLLOWING AFTERNOON, while making herself a cup of green tea, River realized she had forgotten to get her mail on Saturday. She slid her bare feet into some old sandals inside the front door and walked outside.

As she approached her mailbox, she studied its growing mural. Although the painting was still in progress, the scene promised to be quite pretty. In addition to the floral and wildlife details that were taking shape, River noticed with approval that the *E* in *E. Carter* had been painted over with more than one coat of white, and now stood in readiness for the "R" to come. Pleased with the outside of the mailbox, she opened the metal flap to reveal what was inside.

The mailbox was empty.

It had been weeks now, and there had been no reply from Hannah. Had her letter meant anything at all to Hannah, or had Hannah just wondered why River was bothering her after so many years had gone by?

I kind of wonder myself, thought River. *Except I know why: I had no choice. Apparently, for some reason, God wanted that message written and sent to her.*

That was fine. River was fairly certain there was much she had yet to learn about God's ways.

River returned to the house, slipped off her sandals, and, taking her cup of green tea, sat back down with her book. She soon forgot everything else except what was on the page before her.

Chapter Thirty-Three

MAYBE IT WAS the relaxation. Or maybe it was for one of a million other reasons. But that night, when River laid her head on her pillow to sleep, another memory returned: It was one that had been completely lost to her, and now was returned like a necklace unexpectedly brought up from the bottom of the ocean and handed over to its original owner.

Hannah had tried to apologize to her.

River's mouth almost fell open as she remembered. She knew the memory was true. It belonged to her just as surely as her own hands did. How could she have ever forgotten that?

And then, as the rest of the returning memory unfolded, River recalled how, instead of accepting Hannah's apology gracefully and with humility, she had swept it aside, saying an apology wasn't necessary.

River realized that by failing to accept Hannah's apology, River had been the one to leave the wall between them—a barrier that River had denied even existed.

Great, thought River. *This is worse than I had even remembered. Not only did I somehow fail to be there for Hannah in the way she needed in the first place; I also failed her when she tried to make her way back to me.*

Why couldn't a passel of good *memories come back?*, River wondered, directing the question to no one. Instead, here was just more pain—useless and disruptive.

River ran the old scene over once more in her mind, re-processing the information and feeling the impressions that had been entirely lost to her for so long. It was all there. And River had no idea what to do with it.

When the sun rose the next morning, River had slept—badly—for only a couple of hours.

It was probably a good thing Mondays were usually slow days at the shop, thought River. She felt barely fit for human interaction.

She forced herself through every part of her daily routine, behaving like a person, but feeling very little like one.

As soon as it was closing time, she locked the shop, went straight home, and went to bed.

Chapter Thirty-Four

BY DAWN THE following day, River felt more like facing the world. Nothing about the situation had changed, but sleep had made a big difference.

When River opened her email that morning, she found the new logo designs from the graphic artist. They all looked good, and River felt her spirit lift a little bit inside her.

Any one of these would look beautiful on a sign over the door. Her friend had done excellent work, as usual. Surely, one of these could be *the one.*

Now, all River needed to do was figure out *which* one that was, and then she could move forward with getting it on her website, and to Natalie for the Guild website.

Chapter Thirty-Five

IT HAD BECOME one of River's habits to do something uplifting for someone else when she herself was in need of some encouragement. She thought of how much she had enjoyed the muffins Kate had brought her, and decided that she would get one of Kate's recipes and make a batch of the pumpkin-spiced treats to share with Vera and maybe Aunt Della and Uncle Jim, too.

Kate was glad to text River links to both of the recipes she had used, with advice to not fill the muffin cups more than half full or the centers of the muffins would never get done.

On Wednesday, after she closed the shop, River drove out to the food market to get the ingredients for the pumpkin spice muffins, and some muffin papers. It had been a long time since she had baked anything requiring paper goods.

The recipe proved to be a quick and easy one, and soon River had a cooling rack on her counter, lined with the delicious-smelling harbingers of fall.

She gave her project a taste-test for dessert that evening, and, satisfied with the results, packed up several in a bag for Vera and more in another bag for Aunt Della and Uncle Jim. Her gift certainly wasn't anything Aunt Della couldn't easily make for herself—locally famous cook that she was—but maybe, River thought, Della would enjoy eating something she *hadn't* made herself.

River decided she would leave early in the morning and drop these off to their intended recipients.

Chapter Thirty-Six

RIVER WAS SURPRISED to see a crew of roofers at work on the highest peaks of the café when she arrived early the following morning. She hadn't realized that Aunt Della and Uncle Jim were undertaking a roof project. Tarps were spread carefully around the foundation of the house, in an effort to protect Aunt Della's mums and pansies from annihilation. River hoped they would be spared. It would be a pity for a whole season's worth of growth, with its beautiful resulting blooms, to be spoiled in one day by falling debris.

After ascertaining that she would not be in the path of any falling shingles, River strode quickly from her car to the door. Inside the café sat Mr. Lyle, a cup of coffee and a plate of eggs and bacon on the table in front of him.

"Good morning, Mr. Lyle," River said, in neighborly greeting.

"Good morning, Miss Carter," he returned. River was surprised; she hadn't even known he knew who she was. And his greeting seemed downright friendly. Aunt Della's coffee could have that effect on people. She wondered how long it would be until his civility wore off—and then chided herself for her uncharitable thought.

Just then Aunt Della emerged from the kitchen into the front dining area, drying her hands on a towel.

"Oh, my dear, what a nice surprise!" she enthused to River. "Is everything alright?"

"Yeah," said River, realizing that her showing up unannounced first thing in the morning had invited the question. "I just wanted to drop off these muffins to you and Uncle Jim. They're pumpkin spice. I made them last night."

"Ooh," said Aunt Della, taking the bag and peeking inside with a delighted smile. "I might just have to pour myself a cup of coffee and have one of those right now."

"Well, have two," said River. "I made them short so the middles would get done. That's what Kate said to do."

Aunt Della nodded. "I think I could be persuaded to eat two," she laughed.

"Where's Uncle Jim?" asked River.

"Oh, he's outside keeping an eye on this roofing project," she said. "He was probably in the back yard when you came in. He roofed these buildings himself the first two times, you know. But, this time, I told him, 'Jim, the last thing we need is you falling off a roof. Leave that job to the younger ones.' And my brother didn't argue one bit. He just picked up the phone and called someone else to do it. But he'll be out there all day watching, you can be sure of that."

"Will they be done in one day?" River asked. "With this big roof plus Uncle Jim's house?"

"That's what they say," Della replied. "I guess with that many workers at once, it's out with the old and in with the new, all between sunrise and sunset."

Just then two couples entered the café, so River gave her great-aunt a quick hug goodbye.

"Thanks, honey, for the treats. You have a good day," said Aunt Della, who then tucked the bag behind the checkout counter and then headed for the newly occupied tables to take breakfast orders.

As River made her way to her car, the scraping and thumping noises of old shingles being removed filled the air.

ॐ

When River pulled into Vera's driveway, that lady, who appeared to be dressed up for a meeting, was outside on the front step, locking her front door with a key.

"Hello," called River, leaning over from the driver's side to speak through the lowered passenger side window.

"Why, River, how nice to see you," Vera smiled, as she came down her curved front steps to the driveway where River sat inside her car.

"I can see you're headed out, so I won't delay you. I just wanted to drop off these pumpkin spice muffins I made for you."

River stretched over and handed the bag of muffins out the open window.

"Well, what a nice surprise!" said Vera. "Thank you!"

Vera explained that she was driving to another town for the day to help celebrate a friend's birthday.

"If you don't mind, I think I'll take these with me and share them with her."

River said she thought that was a great idea, and wished Vera a good trip.

"Thank you, River. It will be good to see her. We've known each other a long time—since school, in fact. Thanks, again."

With a smile, Vera carried the small parcel up the driveway to her car.

Maintaining long-term friendships seems to have been easier for an earlier generation, thought River, as she ratcheted her neck around to check traffic before backing her car out onto the street.

Such long-lived relationships certainly weren't the norm anymore. River wondered if that really had to do with how the Information Age and the Experience Age had reshaped lifestyles, as one so often heard, or if some other factor was at work.

Chapter Thirty-Seven

BY THE TIME Saturday morning rolled around, River had made a list of things she wanted to look for at the farmers market. Kate laughed at her good naturedly as she excitedly rattled off a wish list that included apple butter, some handmade candles, and a basket to hold her teabags.

"What do you think this market is, Little House on the Prairie?"

"Um, maybe?" River acknowledged.

"Well, you actually *can* probably find all of that stuff," Kate admitted.

"What are you looking for today?" asked River.

"Ah, acorn squash, sweet potatoes, pumpkins, and maybe some collard greens," said Kate.

"So," said River, "I'm feathering my nest, and you're cooking."

"That's about the size of it."

Both women had to be back at their respective stores in time for opening that day, but the deadline didn't dampen their enjoyment one bit.

The early fall air was soft, the light was golden, and the temperatures required only a light jacket. It was the perfect day for strolling through the outdoor market and taking in the sights and scents of the fully stocked booths. They each gradually found the items on their respective lists—and a few more.

"Okay, I take back what I said about Little House on the Prairie," laughed Kate, as they came to a beekeeper's stall featuring honey—and beeswax candles. "Here you go."

When they got to a stand displaying pumpkins and gourds in all sizes, shapes, and a surprising array of colors, Kate said, "You know, I was just planning on getting a pumpkin to eat, but now that I see all of these, I'm thinking maybe I should also get some to decorate the inside of the woodworking shop for AutumnFest."

"I guess I need to think about that, too," said River, "and probably sooner rather than later."

"Well," said Kate, shifting her parcels in her arms so she could check her phone, "I think we have time. We could drop all of this stuff off at the car and come back here. I think we've come around a big loop, so the car isn't that far from this booth."

River agreed, and the two women set off at a brisk pace for the car. After unloading their finds, they set back out for the pumpkin booth. It took two more trips for each of them to carry a selection of various sizes of pumpkins—most orange, some white, and a few warty orange and green ones that captured River's eye because they reminded her of glazed pottery. They also each selected a bag of assorted yellow, green, orange, and white gourds. Every possible variety seemed to be represented—smooth and bumpy; squat, round, and long-necked; striped and solid.

On the drive back to their shops, they chattered excitedly about the prospect of decorating their shops yet that morning. Since they were running later than they had planned, Kate offered to take River straight to her shop, and drive her home later so they could unload the rest of her purchases at her house.

ᘐ

It had been fun to get out and enjoy such a refreshing change of pace, River thought, as she wandered around her shop later that morning, strategically placing pumpkins and gourds to maximize their artistic effect. And she appreciated Kate's easygoing sense of humor. She thought about Kate's take on her shopping list as being worthy of the Ingalls family. The recollection made her laugh. River found it a welcome sound.

She thought about Vera's trip to visit a longtime friend, and wondered if she—River—even knew what it took to build the kind of friendship that could thrive for that long. She always had a good time with Kate when they were together, but they really didn't know each other that well, thought River. Hannah, on the other hand, had known River well. And, yet, that hadn't been enough. What was the missing ingredient?

Chapter Thirty-Eight

IT WAS SUNDAY afternoon before River remembered she hadn't checked her mail on Saturday.

The day was chilly, with tiny drops of cold rain blowing sideways into her face as she made a run for the end of the lane, wishing she had put on some thicker layers for even such a quick voyage.

She reached her hand into the box, grabbed an envelope, and, shielding her head as well as she could with her bent elbow, made a run back for her warm house.

Once inside, she took a look at the rain-spattered envelope. The address was written in tall letters with swooping loops, all with a backward slant. She recognized the handwriting immediately, even though it had been years since she had seen it. She slid out the enclosed note.

Hannah wrote that she had received River's letter and was sorry to hear about her grandmother's passing.

And that was all it said.

Chapter Thirty-Nine

RIVER FELT WORSE now than she had before. Apparently, Hannah hadn't even cared about receiving an apology.

River felt as if she had been pushed—goaded—by the Holy Spirit into reopening communication with Hannah—and for what?

What had been the point? River couldn't see one. It seemed like all that one-ounce envelope had contained was a little more pain. Hannah had not said even one word about the matter of forgiveness. Did she not *want* to forgive? Could she just not be bothered to make the effort? What had any of this accomplished?

And then it struck River: *This* is what it felt like to not be forgiven.

In that moment, River realized in her gut just how deeply *she* had failed Hannah when Hannah had asked River for forgiveness.

River let herself fully realize the truth: Hannah had hurt her deeply. And River had shoved the matter aside with the untrue words, "There's nothing to forgive." But there had been.

River had been so focused recently on seeking forgiveness for how *she* had hurt Hannah, that she hadn't grasped the depth of how Hannah had hurt *her*. The memory washed over River. She remembered how she hadn't seen it coming. It had hit her as unexpectedly as a freight train emerging from a forest where there weren't even any train tracks. The feelings, now years old and previously forgotten, once again ran hard over her.

River had tried to just put it all behind her and keep it there. She guessed that strategy could be called *forgetting*. But she saw now how that strategy hadn't served her well in the long run.

River had become someone who was reluctant to make friends because she thought she didn't know how to be a good one. After all, how could she expect to be a better friend to someone else than she had been to Hannah, whom she had failed, when River didn't even know how she could have done things any differently?

There would always be another shoe, ready to drop—and no woman knew the day or hour of its falling. Eventually, somehow, she would let them down. Who knew when River would do, or say—or fail to do or say—something that would be the last straw for someone she hadn't even realized was counting straws? Or worse—it wouldn't be something she *did*. They would get to know her well enough to find that she *was* someone they didn't want.

No, the *forgetting* strategy had definitely not done her any favors, River decided. And it was off the table anyway, now that she had remembered.

River laid the envelope and the note on the kitchen counter, walked into her unlit bedroom, and lay down on top of the covers of her bed.

"Is this what you had in mind when you had me write that letter?" she silently asked God. "What *is* the point?"

She lay there, waiting, listening, until it was dark outside.

And then she got up and went to the kitchen to heat a cup of chicken bone broth. She wasn't even hungry, but she thought it would warm her up and hopefully help her sleep to have something in her stomach.

As she sat at her kitchen table and slowly drank the golden liquid from a big mug, absently thinking about how healing the drink was supposed to be, something slowly dawned on River: She had not *been* forgiven, but neither had *she* forgiven.

She *still* needed to forgive Hannah for hurting *her*.

River's mug was empty. She held its still-warm ceramic body in her two hands, resting it on the table top. She stared at nothing, while her mind continued to work.

I don't even know how to forgive.

She remained still. It dawned on her that maybe Hannah didn't know how to do it, either. Maybe, like River, her friend didn't even know what forgiveness *was,* let alone how to do it.

Maybe we just try to forget, thought River, *when what we need to know is how to forgive.*

Chapter Forty

THAT NIGHT, RIVER slept the kind of sleep that is thin as tissue and restless and feels like being awake all night, except worse.

When she awoke, it was too early to get up, but there was no possibility of more sleep. She lay there and looked at the curtains in her bedroom. Grandma Ella had made them. Grandma Ella had made so much. She had made a whole life in this place.

River felt empty. Hannah's note, while not containing what River had hoped for, had been right about one thing: Grandma was gone. And now all of Grandma's beautiful pottery pieces were almost gone, too. And nothing would ever replace either.

Maybe this wasn't my calling, thought River.

It had definitely been Grandma's calling. Every part of her life had rung with authenticity, with purpose. In a post-industrial age when craftspeople such as Ella Carter seemed no longer vital for the creation of the functional necessities of daily life, River's grandma had never once doubted her gifts or her call. She was a potter.

River wondered if she, too, *really* had that same calling. Right now, all she seemed to have was memories. And the ones that had recently washed over her all came with jagged edges that cut at her and hurt her soul.

Feeling an uncomfortable weight on her, River put herself through the motions of getting ready, and then left the house before the hummingbirds were even awake.

Chapter Forty-One

WHEN RIVER PULLED up in front of Aunt Della's, the café was dark, but lights shone in the main house. River had texted her great-aunt briefly that morning, so Della was expecting her.

River walked up the short hill to the residence entrance and knocked. Aunt Della opened the big pine door with a smile and invited River to sit down at the kitchen table. A pan of something delicious-smelling was already there, waiting for them.

"Help yourself to the stuffed baked squash, I'm trying a new recipe. Would you like coffee?"

River gratefully accepted on both counts. The mornings were getting cooler, and a warm breakfast was as welcome as the sweaters she had recently unpacked.

She apologized for such an early visit on Della's day off.

"It's quite alright," said Della. "I'm always up and around at the usual time on Mondays. And, anyway, you're welcome any time."

Della set a heavy mug on the table in front of River and poured coffee. "Something on your mind?"

"I just wondered," said River, swallowing a bite of the squash and picking up her coffee, "if there might happen to be any more pieces of Grandma's pottery stored here?"

"That's a good question," said Della thoughtfully. "If there were, they would probably be in that storage room over the café. I'll go check."

River protested that she didn't need to do it right then. But her great-aunt was already en route. "It will only take a minute," she called. "You sit tight."

As River obeyed, she let her eyes roam over the homey kitchen, and her mind went to the past. She remembered childhood visits here, in this house that hadn't changed. Memory, she thought, was both fragile and resilient—like pottery.

She could close her eyes and transport herself back through the years to another morning when she had sat at this very table, eating cereal and listening to her grandma and Aunt Della talk. The two sisters had shared the same laugh.

River remembered how her feet had dangled as she had sat in the grownup-sized chair.

Today, her feet rested solidly on the wood floor. And everything in this familiar kitchen appeared smaller than her childhood memory had recorded it.

River was still welcomed and loved in this home, but she was no longer a tiny visitor in the Valley of Artisans. She was a grown woman, with a life of her own here—a calling.

Just then, Della breezed back into the kitchen.

"I didn't find any there," she reported. "But I'll send Jim to check the attic when he gets back. He and Sara left early to go to Indy for art supplies. I expect he'll be back by late afternoon. I'll call you."

River took in the information about Great-Uncle Jim's whereabouts without comment, and thanked her aunt for her help and the delicious breakfast. She swallowed the last of her coffee, hugged Aunt Della, and headed out for her shop.

Chapter Forty-Two

PUTTING THE LEATHER sandal keychain back into her bag, River stepped inside her shop and turned on the lights.

In that moment, it struck her that the place looked exactly as it had when River was a child. All of the remaining pieces lining the shelves were Grandma's work. All of the wall hangings were just as grandma had left them.

River had taken ownership of Grandma's *house*—putting her own touches on it so that it no longer looked just the same as it had when River was younger. But she had not fully taken hold of her place as the owner of the pottery shop. She had left everything about the shop as it was—not even adding any of her own pieces to the store. She had made no new pieces in the months she had been here, and she hadn't even unpacked her own pottery that she'd brought with her. And she still hadn't completed the name change.

River looked over at the still, empty wheel. It had been just keyboards and meetings instead of clay for... how long? She caught sight of her short, neat fingernails, and the thought struck her that they were too clean for happiness.

I haven't been using my creative gifts, thought River. *And that's a big reason I've been feeling badly.*

"You've been focusing on doing what you had to do to run a successful business," she told herself.

But I've been stuffing down my need to create, she thought. *I've deprived myself of what I really love and was put here to do, until I nearly reduced life to a series of motions to be gone through from morning until night. No wonder I'm not full of life and peace and joy. This is my soul, telling me it is hungry.*

She was now the proprietor of a pottery shop, and a meaningful contributor to a community of artisans. But *what* had she been contributing? Everything *except* her art—which was the heart of her, and would be the heart of her shop.

She had been living *from* the past, instead of letting the past take its rightful place. To embrace this life—or even feel like she was living it—she was going to have to *make pottery.*

When Aunt Della called to say that Uncle Jim had found more of Grandma's pottery in the attic, and did she want him to bring it over, River thanked them both for their trouble, and asked Della to please keep it.

River was ready. She would make her own pieces to restock the store.

Chapter Forty-Three

RIVER SET TO work. First, she would pack up all of Grandma's pottery tools from the workroom, and bring in her own tools, which were still sitting in a box in the garage.

Grandma's worn and discolored tools were arranged neatly on pegboard on the wall. The row of potter's needles was first, bookended by hooks holding chamois clothes, towels, and Grandma's apron. A second row of hooks across the bottom of the pegboard held the fettling knives, cut-off wires, and an assortment of brushes.

There was nothing wrong with Grandma's tools, nothing wrong with them at all, thought River, as she carefully took each one down and wrapped it. But, to River, they would always be Grandma's, and nothing could change that. For River to fully step into her place here, she would need to use her own tools. They would be practically identical to Grandma's—and they could hang on the same hooks. But they would serve as extensions of her, of River Carter, not of Ella Carter.

As soon as River had wrapped and boxed the last of Ella's well-worn instruments, she strode out of the workroom to the table behind the counter. She sat down and turned on her laptop just long enough to place a rush order for clay and some of her favorite pottery glazes. Thankfully, there was a supplier nearby. *Not surprising*, River thought, *considering southern Indiana is pretty much made of clay.*

That done, she smacked the computer lid shut and dialed Vera's number.

Chapter Forty-Four

IT WAS TIME to get forgiveness figured out. Another night like last night would be one more than enough.

As soon as River had resolved to do something about it—though she didn't know what—Vera's name had popped into her mind.

Vera had said she always had time for her best friend's granddaughter and that, in fact, if River was free that evening, why didn't she come over then. And now, here they were, sitting on Vera's screened-in porch, as the evening sun continued its steady trek toward the bottom of the sky.

It had almost been as if Vera had been expecting her call. But, of course, thought River, that was impossible.

Vera was the kind of person who seemed to look into your soul and then just started right there. Small talk wasn't really in her vocabulary, and neither were platitudes. But there was something in her eyes that let you know you were safe. The phrase "speak the truth in love" flitted across River's mind like a swallowtail butterfly. Yes, that was it. And it was exactly what River needed.

They sat in the fading light and River told Vera about how, as her brain continued to heal, she was receiving back many of her own lost memories. Some had come back in parts, incomplete and out of order, weeks or months apart. And some had brought pain with them. She told Vera about Hannah.

"I'm stuck," River confessed. "I've done all I know how to do, but it's not enough. I don't have peace."

She didn't have to tell Vera that she was still in pain. She could see that Vera knew that was why she was here—although River didn't really know what Vera could do to help.

When River stopped talking, Vera sat quietly for a moment before speaking. Somewhere outside, a windchime softly sent its music into the air.

Vera's words, when they came, were gentle, yet filled with authority and the ring of truth. She helped River realize that she had done all she could do in the matter of *asking* for forgiveness. And that, regarding the wrong Hannah had done *to* her, River did not have to remain in the hurt she had remembered.

"You can forgive the other person, without even telling that person anything about it," Vera continued, "and that forgiveness will free both of you spiritually."

River's face must have registered her puzzled reaction.

"Forgiving someone," Vera explained, "even someone who hasn't asked for forgiveness, sets both parties free in a very real way, sometimes with surprising results."

"Okay, but how do I actually do that?" River asked.

Vera spoke simply, and her words were like a light leading River through a cave.

"Hannah did owe you something real. You can put a name on what she owed you. And, so, you do that. Name the debt. And then you release that person from that debt by handing it over to God. If it helps, envision an actual IOU with words written on it, and yourself transferring ownership of the paper to God. Once you have made the decision to do that, the debt is no longer yours to hold.

"You see," Vera continued, "you have acknowledged the reality that it was a *real* debt—you're not denying that the other person owed it and never paid it. But you are *forgiving* that debt—even if the other person isn't sorry, even if they never realize their actions were hurtful. And when you transfer ownership of the debt to God, you are placing that person into God's hands for *his forgiveness*, as well. This will free you—and them."

"Okay, but then how do I forget?" asked River.

"Forgiveness is not dependent on forgetting," said Vera. "Forgiveness has everything to do with *remembering*—remembering the freedom of forgiveness God offers us—and the freedom that we receive when we forgive others."

"But what do I do about Hannah not forgiving me?" River asked softly.

"Friends are a gift from God, and they can be very important in life. But real wholeness and peace will come to you from God, not people," said Vera. "Pray for your friend. Ask God to soften her heart so she can recognize her unforgiveness and confess it to him, so that he can heal her heart."

So that's it, thought River. *I no longer need anything from Hannah to make me whole. God is the one who does that.*

River closed her eyes for a minute to think about all Vera had said, and then to do it.

An involuntary sigh silently left her. River knew that something real had just been accomplished.

"Now," said Vera, "if you would like, I will pray for your physical healing. It seems like you have come a long way, but not all the way."

"Yes, please," River said quietly.

The prayer that Vera prayed was not like any prayer for healing that River had heard before. But she found herself trusting this woman. She noticed that Vera's quiet authority also had a bolstering effect on her own faith.

After the prayer, River stood and picked up her bag and thanked Vera for all of her help.

"How did you learn all of this?" River asked.

"I needed wisdom, so I asked God for it," Vera replied simply.

That night River slept soundly, not even waking once until her alarm clock sounded.

Chapter Forty-Five

RIVER'S HEART QUICKENED the next morning as she approached the pottery shop and saw that the clay and glazes had already been delivered. She quickly opened the front door with the familiar key, then wrestled the heavy boxes inside using both her hands and her feet.

She glanced around at all of the nearly empty display shelves that would need to be full before the festival. Instead of feeling daunted, she found that she was excited about filling them.

River went back out to her car to retrieve the box of her own pottery tools she'd brought, and unpacked and put them away in her workroom.

She did some quick calculating on her phone to figure out how many pieces she would need to make in all, and how many of those would need to be made each day.

She could do it. It would mean dedicated hours six days a week, but it could be done. And River knew that it must be done, because the income from in-store sales during the festival would carry her through those times when there weren't as many customers in the shop. She thought of her great-uncle's remark, and silently agreed with him: Since she didn't plan to give up her habit of eating any time soon, she was going to need to make money.

Relishing the silence that filled the little shop, River rolled up her sleeves, sat down at the old wheel that she had used many times when Grandma had been here, and began making her own pottery.

Her thoughts moved as fluidly and gently as the wet clay under her fingers. Like the vase that emerged between her cupped left hand and the fingers of her right hand, the realization formed inside her that she felt more alive than she had in a long time.

Her soul had been hungry. And this, it was letting her know, was its preferred sustenance. This, somehow, was what gave life to her spirit.

This *was* River Carter's Pottery Works, she thought, as she watched the clay intently and carefully orchestrated its shaping on the moving wheel. It wasn't so because she had happened to inherit a business from someone, but because this was her destiny. This was what she had been born to do, and her whole life had been preparing her to do it. She *would* do it.

As her spirit rose up closer to its full height, an idea came to River: She would not just make the standard fare that people expected—mugs and vases. She *would* make those things; she liked them as much as she knew others did, and she enjoyed making them. But she would also take more artistic risks. She would make pieces that people didn't even know they might like until they saw them, but that, once seen, would speak deeply to them of the stunning beauty of creation.

Ideas now seemed to flow to River one after another, as they had not done in years. They proceeded like a parade moving past a grandstand, each one pausing to be considered before moving on to make way for the next.

She would make unique pieces that would evoke people's best memories of the season. She would use the deep, rich earth tones she loved and for which fall in Indiana was known. She would take her cues from the kaleidoscope of changing autumn leaves and of the ever-expanding variety of pumpkins and gourds; and from the array of deep, rich reds, yellows, oranges, bronzes, creams, and various purples of chrysanthemums.

She would make large pieces, such as oversized serving bowls and plates and pitchers that could grace dining tables all fall, right through Thanksgiving.

And she would also make small pieces, such as mug covers, teabag caddies, whimsical salt and pepper sets, and decorative spoon rests, all with just as much color and character as the larger items.

She could do this for every season of the year, River realized with a thrill. She could develop entire collections of functional pottery based around the beauty of nature, not just in fall, but in winter, spring, and summer. And the collection wouldn't stop at tableware.

Just then, a concept for a jewel-toned summer collection inspired by the hummingbirds made her heart do a little winged flit of its own. She envisioned a stunning pitcher and vases, as well as hummingbird-themed decorative wall hooks for robes and necklaces, and a hummingbird ringholder in which the bird's beak did the work. Why not try a decorative light switch cover while she was at it?

She mentally reviewed the various glaze tones she could use for the summer collection, foremost among them, the shiny iridescent greens and blues that also reminded her of the peacocks she had seen at the zoo during childhood visits. That thought led her to consider still other shimmering living subjects for her creative work, such as dragonflies and June bugs. River quickly dismissed the beetle idea, however, preferring not to focus on a creature that seemed so bent on destruction. The circle of life might be part of nature, but she firmly resolved that not every aspect of it needed to be featured in her art.

She continued to work quietly at the wheel for several hours as the parade of ideas proceeded, interrupted.

River could not have pinpointed the exact moment when the shift had occurred, but at some point during the morning, she realized that something was different. The old hurt that she had thought was just part of her now didn't hurt anymore. It seemed to have become an objective memory. She hadn't forgotten it; she knew that there had been pain. But it didn't hurt in the present anymore. It no longer had a life of its own.

Chapter Forty-Six

RIVER DIDN'T REALLY want to stop for lunch, but she knew it wasn't a good idea to stay at the wheel nonstop for a whole day. She knew from experience that it was better to give the body a break. Also, she was hungry.

She was glad for the leftovers she had packed that morning, and for the ancient mini-microwave in the back room. Salads had been fine when the weather had been warm, but, lately, warm food had seemed like more the thing. A sliced tomato could be a refreshing cooler in the late summer, but once the chill of fall arrived, River preferred that same tomato pureed with warm bone broth and herbs to make a nourishing soup.

As she ate her soup, she steeped some green tea to fill her travel mug. She would take it along with her and go stretch her legs. She would walk down to the gazebo and back; it would be good to get some sunshine and to say hello to Kate.

River was able to accomplish two of her three objectives. Kate hadn't been in the woodworking shop when she had popped in. Danny said that she had gone out to pick up their lunch and that River was welcome to wait for her. But River was too eager to get back to the shop and continue her work. She also knew that, while Danny's polite invitation was sincere, he was busy trying to get more pieces made for the woodworking shop the same way she was trying to get more pottery pieces made for her own store. She knew that every fifteen-minute block of time counted—for both of them. So, rather than waiting, she thanked Danny and said she would catch up with Kate later.

Back at her shop, River composed a short but triumphant email to her graphic designer, letting her know that the new name of the pottery shop would be *River Carter's Pottery Works*, and asking if she would please revise and send the necessary files for the new logo.

Then, returning to her wheel, River settled in once more to create. Inspired by all things autumnal, she began making a new piece. It would be a soup bowl shaped like a pumpkin with the top cut out. Its handle would be a green pumpkin vine, while the pumpkin itself would be a deep orange. The bowl would be part of a set that would be both whimsical and functional, River decided.

She would make similarly sized bowls in various colors and patterns, and people could either buy them individually, or pick and choose whichever ones they liked to make a set. She would make a dark green one fashioned after an acorn squash, and a cream one with green and orange stripes, evocative of the pattern on a delicata squash. She might also make a golden yellow one inspired by spaghetti squash. River didn't even realize that she was smiling as she envisioned the finished pieces.

River nearly had the first soup bowl formed, when the wheel stopped. It had given no warning at all. It just stopped.

River was so surprised that she placed her hands, still covered in wet clay, on her hips, as she stared at the machine.

This was no time for the wheel to break. Now what would she do? She had already calculated how many pieces she needed to make each day to be ready for the festival. Downtime was not in the schedule.

While living with her parents in Tennessee, River had used her mother's wheel. But using it, even for a short time, wasn't an option now. Her mother was a working potter, too, and needed her own wheel to stay right where it was. This wasn't the time of year that any potter could spare their wheel.

River knew it would cost over a thousand dollars to get a new one, and she just didn't have that at the moment. Now was the time her business needed to bring in money, not spend it.

River took her cutting wire and carefully cut the clay bowl off the wheel with practiced hands, leaving it in place. It wasn't ready to be lifted off yet, or else its shape would be distorted. It would need to stay there a while to dry.

She could still see in her mind's eye the beautiful variety of colorful squash bowls she had imagined, but the bowl in front of her would not become one of them, after all. It could still be a good bowl, but it would be a smooth one without a handle, rather than the pumpkin River had envisioned. She put a cover over it to help the clay dry properly.

River stared at the wheel. It felt like a chasm had opened between where she had been headed, and where she currently was.

How would she get from here to there with a broken wheel?

Chapter Forty-Seven

AS SHE WASHED her hands at the work sink, staring at the muddy water run onto the white ceramic, River's thoughts went to the newly found stash of Grandma's finished pieces sitting safely in Great-Aunt Della's attic.

With one call to her aunt, she could have more of Grandma's pieces to restock her shop for the festival.

But, as River considered that option, the excitement she had felt that morning began to dry and shrivel. Something good that had been tall inside her earlier in the day begin to fold down and close up.

What should she do?

And then River remembered something Vera had said.

When River had asked Vera how she had learned the things she knew, Vera had said that she asked God.

If God had shown Vera such things when she asked him for wisdom, why wouldn't he show River what to do in this situation if she asked him?

River wanted to. She wanted there to be a better way forward than the only way she could think of on her own. The way she could think of made her feel like she was going backward instead of forward. The only way she could imagine already felt to her like living someone else's life, instead of the one she now realized she had been put here to live.

Rather than call Aunt Della to ask for Grandma's stored pottery, River decided she would ask God to show her what to do.

Chapter Forty-Eight

AS OFTEN HAPPENS during autumn in Indiana, summer made an encore visit the next morning. It was unusually bright, and all of the colors outside—of the red mums, the orange pumpkins, the red maple trees, and the blue sky—appeared intensely vibrant.

It was lovely and warm and comfortable, the kind of beautiful fall day that makes people smile and feel good, and River did. She didn't want to miss being out in it. One really didn't know how many more of those there might be, and that fact alone made them precious. Not to mention that the freedom of being comfortable outside in a short-sleeved shirt and sandals—with no weighty layers needed—was one River held dear.

As undeniably gorgeous as the morning was, however, the matter of the wheel remained unresolved. And so, as she sat at the patio table in the backyard, eating her breakfast of coconut kefir and berries, River was thinking about her predicament.

The evening before, she had asked God to show her what to do. She knew that God was already aware of the urgency of the situation, but she had reminded him, anyway. And then she had poured out her heart.

She told him that the only solution she could think of for her current predicament involved moving backward instead of forward, and that she didn't want to just slide back into running Ella Carter's pottery shop. She did not want to live in the past—hers or anyone else's—and she did not want to exist in the shadow of someone else's destiny. She wanted to become who she had been made to be. She wanted to live River Carter's life—the one she had been uniquely designed to live, doing the things she had been destined by God to do.

She told him how grateful she was for the positive changes that she knew had come to her after she and Vera had prayed. She told him she knew that she was already freer and more complete than she had been just two days before. And she thanked him for what he was doing.

River had meant every word, and it had felt good to just lay it all out like that.

She wondered how quickly God had gotten back with Vera after she asked him for wisdom. She also wished she had thought to ask Vera how the answer had come. The way Vera had put it, so matter-of-factly, one might have thought that she had just sat in a tent and talked with God face to face as he had talked to Moses, and that he had told her in so many words. River guessed, however, that it probably had happened some other way.

Just then, one of Emerald's hummingbird associates—one about two-thirds his size—flew near the patio table. River directed her full attention to the black and jewel-colored creature. It looked like the one she had named Simon. He didn't seem to be particularly focused on anything other than the pure enjoyment of flying.

She remembered how, on the night of the cookout, a hummingbird like this one—or maybe it had been this same one—had entertained them all with his flying antics. The memory unexpectedly made River laugh.

It was in that moment, without notice or fanfare, that a memory from River's childhood came to her in vivid detail, as if she were seeing it on a screen.

A young River had been watching Grandma Ella do something to the potter's wheel, and had asked her what she was doing. Grandma had explained matter-of-factly, "The wheel head is stuck to the shaft, so I'm removing it to put some anti-seize grease on it."

River had watched as Grandma put the little bottle of grease back in its place in a cupboard in the workroom.

"Now the wheel can fly again," Grandma had said. And the child River had laughed at the idea of a wheel actually flying.

That was it. River knew without a doubt that this was the answer to the current wheel problem. She could hardly wait to get to the pottery shop.

She finished her breakfast hurriedly, gathered up her utensils from the table, and took them inside the house. In the kitchen, she poured the rest of her hot tea into a travel mug, quickly pulled some leftovers from the refrigerator and set them into her lunch cooler, and collected the rest of her things.

She had planned to ride her bike today, to enjoy the beautiful weather and the smell of leaves and the sound of already-spent acorns crunching under her tires, but now she felt like she couldn't bear the suspense of the extra time it would take to get there. She would roll the car windows down instead, she told herself, as she rushed toward the garage.

Arriving at the pottery shop, River unlocked the door, not even stopping to turn the ceramic door sign to *OPEN*. She hurriedly set her tea mug down on the counter and gently lowered all of her bags to one spot on the floor, leaving them there in a pile.

River strode straight to the workroom, and went directly to the cupboard she had seen that morning in her memory. The grease was exactly where she had seen Grandma put it away.

River sat down at the wheel, and, taking her cutting wire in both hands, carefully re-cut yesterday's bowl, now leather-hard, and lifted it off the bat. She moved it to a drying cabinet.

River then did everything exactly as she had recalled Grandma Ella doing it all those years ago. She removed the wheel head from the shaft, applied the anti-seize grease, and then put the wheel head back. River took a breath as she flipped the switch.

The potter's wheel began, once again, to fly.

Chapter Forty-Nine

BY THE LAST day of AutumnFest, River had sold more new pottery pieces of her own making than the number of pieces she had made in her entire life up to that point. Her seasonal designs had been a source of delight to visitors and townspeople alike. Word of mouth from both tourists and neighbors had caused her business to grow more quickly than the piles of colored leaves under the many trees in the Valley.

River's parents had come for a visit during the festival, and she could tell they were as thrilled as she was to see her business taking off. They had also loved what she'd done to the front door of her house. No one could remember how long the door had been painted, but they all agreed it was stunning with the true woodgrain showing.

Nick, her brother, hadn't been able to come for AutumnFest because of his class schedule, but Great-Aunt Della had invited the whole family to come for Thanksgiving dinner at her house, and Nick would be here then.

One of the more surprising aspects of AutumnFest, thought River, as she headed home after closing her shop on the last day of the festival, had to be the sign that Mr. Lyle had had made for the front window of his broom shop. *Welcome. Home of AutumnFest*, it declared. From detractor to avid supporter, thought River. She wondered what had been responsible for the change, and whether it might be a harbinger of things to come. Only time would tell.

And I'll be here to see, thought River. *I'll be right here in the Valley, not just* watching *what happens next, but helping to* shape *it*.

River had remembered to make a quick stop on her way home to pick up some goat cheese for the spinach-walnut-cranberry salad that was on the menu that night. Vera and Danny and Kate were all coming over for a carry-in dinner. River had even remembered to take her reusable shopping bag into the store; she had been remembering more and more things ever since Vera had prayed for her healing.

Even though it was still relatively early in the evening, it was already dusk by the time River arrived home. She put her things inside the house and then walked out to her mailbox. In the light of the lamppost, she admired Sara's completed handiwork once again. *R. Carter,* the mailbox now read, the name standing out in black letters on the fresh design of morning glory and moonflower vines, with some colorful new butterflies and hummingbirds added in.

Emerald and Simon and the other hummingbirds had already migrated for winter, but River felt sure they'd be back.

As she opened the mailbox with one finger, River reached inside with her other hand to pull out the one oversized envelope inside.

It was a card, addressed in the distinctive handwriting that could belong to only one person she knew. She really had never expected to see that lettering again, but there it was, with its tall, backward-slanting letters and swooping loops.

A warmth of gratitude rose in her heart for the peace that had become hers, for all of the restoration and healing that God had poured out inside her. Regardless of what was in this envelope, she knew that that wholeness would still be hers. *Whatever is inside this envelope, I surrender it to you, God.*

River tucked the large envelope between her elbow and her side and headed for the house. She would open it later.

Her friends would be here very soon, and she still needed to make that salad.

Visit the Valley of Artisans Again

There is more just waiting for you in the Valley of Artisans series!

Open for Miracles – Book 2
It's WinterFest time in the Valley of Artisans, and River Carter's new life may be about to snowball. Uncle Jim and Sara announce a winter wedding—but will their trip down the aisle end before it begins? And when one of Vera's big prayers for River is answered, will life be the same for any of them again?

A Winter Wedding in the Valley of Artisans – Book 3
The Valley's charming wedding chapel is finally ready for its grand opening. But when an ice storm brings an unexpected wedding guest with questions for River Carter, where will his inquiries lead?

Ordinary Miracles – Book 4
River Carter is unexpectedly faced with a challenge to her very beliefs about how God works. As she transforms her neglected garden into a place of inspiring beauty, will she find herself coming to life in a new way, as well?

Note from the Author

You're invited to join my email community, at https://amylu-riley.com.

Made in the USA
Monee, IL
25 November 2021